Waiting:
stories

Waiting:
stories

Dumitru Tsepeneag

Translated by Patrick Camiller

DALKEY ARCHIVE PRESS
CHAMPAIGN / LONDON / DUBLIN

Originally published in Romanian as *Așteptare* by Cartea Românească, Bucharest, 1971

Copyright © 1971 by Dumitru Tsepeneag
Translation © 2013 by Patrick Camiller

First edition, 2013

Library of Congress Cataloging-in-Publication Data

Tepeneag, Dumitru, 1937-
[Asteptare. English]
Waiting : stories / Dumitru Tsepeneag ; Translated by Patrick Camiller. -- First Edition.
pages cm.
"Originally published in Romanian as Asteptare by Cartea Româneasca, Bucharest, 1971."
ISBN 978-1-56478-901-3 (alk. paper)
I. Title.
PC840.3.E67A913 2013
859'.334--dc23
2013026004

Partially funded by a grant from the Illinois Arts Council, a state agency, and by the Translation and Publication Support Program of the Romanian Cultural Institute

www.dalkeyarchive.com

Cover design and composition by Tim Peters
Cover photo: *Man Sleeping Inside a Tent*, ca. 1900-1909. Herman T. Bohlman Photograph Collection.

Printed on permanent/durable acid-free paper

Contents

Author's Note

The present volume contains a selection of my "youthful" writings (1958–1968), dating from before I embarked upon my first novel (*Vain Art of the Fugue*). I have selected and ordered them in such a way as to correspond to the different stages of life. We spend our entire lives waiting for something, though we never know what. We don't dare tell ourselves that what we are waiting for is death. Read in order, from beginning to end, I would like to think that these texts might hint at a kind of biography. Not mine, but anyone's.

At the Photographer's

I lost patience and went out first. As I waited for the car to arrive, I stamped my feet on the pavement in front of the building. Then Father came out, looking very serious, hands behind his back, in that new navy-blue pinstriped suit. He told me to calm down, to stop bucking around like a baby lamb, but there was nothing reproachful in his voice and he didn't even look at me as he said it. He straightened his hat, checked his tie, and looked again at the street door. He began to walk up and down, hands still behind him, his head slightly bowed, while I, feeling bored, looked at the tram stop and thought that it wasn't so far to the photographer's: just a few meters past the grocery, in an old house that had escaped demolition, across from the place with those nice shiny boxes that people called coffins. It was quite possible to go on foot, but, no, the Princess didn't like the idea of that. "I'll get my train dirty," she said, lifting herself up on tiptoe, so that Father called a taxi. Gigi had a smile on his face and seemed to be looking out the window all the time; he was even taller than usual, and that annoyed me, so I didn't wait for the elevator. When the car arrived there was no sign of Father: he'd gone back up to make them get a move on. The driver pulled up and asked me if he had the right address. "A wedding, is it?" he asked, with a smile and a nod. I hurried to the stairs, but just then the Princess and Gigi, Father and Aunt Luiza, walked out of the lift; they were all laughing and talking at the same time. They took no notice of me, and didn't want to take me with them. It doesn't matter, I said. I let them go on ahead, then dashed off on my own. I knew the way, so I got there before them. At first I was afraid that the photo shoot had gone too quickly and everyone had already left, but that wasn't possible. I still asked the photographer if they'd been there. He scratched his goatee with his long black fingernails and gave me an uncomprehending look. I described my sister to him: how she's fat from eating cakes all day, how she's always putting on airs and graces, how she started to look down her nose at me once she went to university. She wants to get married, I told the photographer. At first Father was against it: he told her to finish studying first, to put something in her head, then they'd see about it. (At that point he'd caught me thumbing my nose at her and banged his fist on the table: "Get out of here, you snotty little brat!") The Princess was beside herself for days on end, crying all the time and, instead of cakes, eating nothing but those hard candies you crunch between your teeth. I also told the photographer about Aunt Luiza, who moved in with us after Mother died. The man kept his eyes on me and stroked his beard, with fingers that looked as if they had been dabbed with walnut stain. God knows what had happened to the other wedding guests. I wanted to go inside and wait for them there, but that goat of a photographer patted me on the head and pushed me back into the street. I ran across to the store with the coffins, to see what was new there, and was nearly run over by a Pobeda; the driver slammed on his brakes and swore at me, but when I stuck my tongue out he shut up and drove off. There was a lovely new coffin in the window, so small that I don't think even I would have fitted into it. I'll have to tell Dan about it at school tomorrow; he likes coffins too, and those wreaths with wide black ribbons and white lettering. But, unlike me, he's never been to the cemetery, and he's thinner than I am. If we start wrestling with each other, I trip him and make him fall and it's all over—only the Princess doesn't believe me and laughs, throwing her head back so that her throat wobbles like a frog's. She cackled like that when Gigi came round the first time and played backgammon with Father; I was on Gigi's side because he sometimes let me roll the dice for him and I always got doubles, until Father lost his temper and told me to put the dice in the shaker. It was then that she burst out laughing. After Gigi left, I asked Father to play backgammon with me—just one game wouldn't have hurt—but he refused and told me to stick to my own games. What could I do? I took the backgammon board and played it on my own, left against right, and the Princess started to laugh again. Look, there she is on the other side of the street, laughing as she climbs out of the car, while Gigi stands stiff as a poker and smiles like a streetlamp. Father and Aunt Luiza are also there on the pavement, as well as another fat person who looks as if she could be a woman. A car has pulled up, and another. Everyone is happy and flapping their arms, as if trying to rise into the air—what a strange crowd! I waited for them all to squeeze into old Goatee's studio, then quickly crossed the street and peered through the window of the half-open door. The Princess was wearing a white dress with all kinds of frills, and had a weird crown on her head. She was flushed, and smiling rather than laughing—as pretty as a picture. Gigi was so tall that the photographer looked up at him as at a streetlamp, his beard shaking as he danced around the couple. They kept growing, in his eyes, as though someone were stretching them by yanking on their hair. I sneaked in, taking care that Father didn't see me, and huddled motionless in a corner. The photographer pulled a red curtain aside, turned on some large lamps shaped like car headlights, then went out the back and returned with his camera and tripod, which towered over me. My sister turned a deeper red, Gigi white as a sheet, while Aunt Luiza took out a handkerchief to wipe away her tears. The others made a terrible din, talking and laughing at the top of their voices, until Goatee finally said: "Silence, please, we're starting to shoot!" I stood on tiptoe to see better, but there was no need, because the bride and groom rose half a meter from the ground and were being pulled higher and higher by strings. No one said anything; only Aunt Luiza sobbed her heart out. The photographer was half-hidden in a box behind the camera, so that only his hands were visible. It became quiet, and a few lowered their heads as if guilty of something—or ashamed. They held themselves stiff. The couple rose higher and higher: you could see their shoes by now, his as large as black boats tapering at the prow, hers smaller and partly covered by the hem of her dress. A shrew of a princess, look how fat, and now rising like a balloon. I cast a sidelong glance at Father: his eyes were moist. Aunt Luiza was still sobbing away, and another lady was crying more softly. Gigi's head was within two inches of the ceiling. The photographer popped out from his box, raised his arms, and yelled: "What are you doing, my friends? You've gone too high: I can't only shoot your lower halves. What a business!" His shouts shook the others from their reverie. I jumped out from my place and was the first to try to catch them by the legs, but I failed. "Give him a hand, will you," the photographer snapped. "Don't just sit there like logs." Everyone started jostling, as in a packed tram, trying to grab one leg or another to pull them down, at first with gentle tugs ("Come down now, that's enough!"), but then heaving with all their strength, in vain. Aunt Luiza was shrieking: "Lord, how shameful! What will people say?" while poor Father, at his wits' end, kept spinning around and telling everyone that he'd always thought they should finish their studies first, and only then . . . I climbed onto a chair and began to chant, as at a football match: "Go for it, Princess, go for it!" Everyone was getting into it now; it was no longer a laughing matter. The bride and groom passed headfirst through the ceiling, sending chunks of plaster and cement onto the people below. After trying without success to point his camera in such a way that he could at least get a shot of their feet, the photographer no longer knew what to do and tugged his goatee in desperation;

never in all his life had he been witness to such willful or shameless behavior. My sister was kicking wildly, wanting to be left alone, she knew what she was doing. Gigi had only one shoe left; a big hulk of a man had tugged on the other one, but he too had given up the struggle in the end. The couple soared up and up, through ceiling, loft, and roof. We all went into the street to figure out their trajectory. "What a disgrace, what nerve! Call the fire brigade!" someone shouted, and it made me want to laugh. I'd crossed the street again to get a better view, and resting against the window with the coffins I followed their progress with delight. They were still rising, hand in hand, just the two of them, and they were finely dressed, and the sky was blue. Good for you, Princess! She wasn't laughing anymore.

The Dead Fish

I was there too, in front of the restaurant, among the onlookers pushing to get a look at the dead fish. Though they kept jostling me and treading on my feet, I couldn't bring myself to leave. My satchel felt heavy on my shoulders; a woman was leaning against it, and she was fat and had a sharp, angry voice.

"What funny people! What a bunch of weirdoes!"

It was early; the restaurant was shut. Three blocks of ice on top of one another, together with a few discarded flowers, lay in the alleyway leading to the kitchen. Next to them, the fish.

"A dead fish, that's all," the woman said, reaching out protectively and taking my hand in hers. It felt hot and sweaty. Her squeaking tone grated on my eardrums.

The glassy eye of the fish stared past us. Its scales were like green fingernails, blue at the edges. It lay facing the gutter, half in the alley, where there was ice, half on the wet asphalt of the sidewalk.

"What's a fish doing on the sidewalk?"

"They must have brought it for the restaurant . . ."

"And so big!"

A tall man, dry as a salted herring, clutching a yellow briefcase under his arm, made his way out of the crowd. He looked distrustful and waved a finger at me in admonishment. Some others took the opportunity to leave.

"A fish . . ."

People shrugged. The woman beside me was still wondering: how could they leave it there like a museum exhibit? And she shook her head reproachfully. Then she brightened up.

"You could put it on a spit, like a calf. It would feed a whole wedding!"

"What a plump little morsel!" someone said, beginning to stroke my hair. "Wouldn't be bad in a fish soup either."

They were joking and chortling, some even licking their chops. It was a workday morning, the sun was only just up. I couldn't make up my mind to leave. Dead like that, it seemed bigger and longer—the size of a man. Its whitish belly was gradually turning mauve; the scales no longer glistened and looked kind of smoky. Only its eyes still had a gleam in them. People were leaving. The woman with the trumpet voice scolded me:

"What are you gawking at there? It's just a dead fish. Haven't you got anything better to do? Shouldn't you be at school?"

Everyone agreed with her, gesticulating and moving their heads up and down in unison. I walked away. But at the street corner I looked to see if the woman was still there, and went back. Not many onlookers were left: a stooped old man, holding a kid by the hand, plus a few others. People were hurrying to work and rarely even stopped, content to cast a sidelong glance in passing. I leaned against the restaurant window and looked at its eye, but it didn't say anything to me. All fish have the same eyes. I didn't dare to touch it. And I didn't know if it was the one, I didn't want it to be—the fish that came to my window in the evening when I was alone. On those days its scales gleamed like amethyst drops. Its fine head with thick lips stuck to the glass pane, and it stayed there with me until the moon rose above the house opposite. When I was sad it danced in front of the window, by the yellow light of the streetlamp. It was a strange dance, heavy and awkward, and sometimes it lost balance and flipped over on its belly, hitting its tail against the post and almost banging the sidewalk with its mouth, but correcting itself in time. I became fond of it and laughed merrily at its pranks. I don't know if the dead fish was the same one. Soon afterward I moved with my parents to another neighborhood, to a big block where we had a balcony. And I liked to go out onto the balcony and look at the city lights, those little golden fishes.

Then I started secondary school.

Insomnia

The wind is making the window frame creak. I must have dozed off. Mechanically, I reach out to feel the wall on my left. It is cold and rough. Boots are pounding in the street, louder and louder. They are resolute steps, the steps of someone who has an order to carry out. I raise myself on my elbows. The pounding suddenly stops. I strain my ears: a weak sound of grating iron and muffled lapping, then silence. The bulb of the streetlamp on the opposite pavement casts a dirty, yellowish light. It is no longer raining. There is a house across the street, without balconies. During the day a fat man appears at one of the windows; he wears a policeman's cap but no jacket, only a shirt with shoulder straps. He has a smile on his face. A church tower can be glimpsed over the rooftops. From where I'm standing, all I can see of the building to my right is one window illuminated by a blood-red light, a little above the level of mine. Again I hear the pounding, quicker than before, as the steps go off into the distance. Sometimes the policeman's daughter, or perhaps his wife, also shows herself. I can't tell if she's pretty; sometimes it seems to me that she is. The pounding has faded away. I usually have a chair to the right of my bed, in place of a night table. I reach out for my cigarettes. My fingers knock against the ashtray. I get up and go to the window. Quite a large fish, with gleaming purple scales, floats around the window frame. It is attached to the jamb by a piece of string or wire and spins at an even speed, like a gramophone disc, always at a distance of about one meter. In the morning you can hear music in the house across the street, from the girl's window. Now it's dark everywhere, except for that window on the right, where they're probably developing photographs and need a red light. It is no longer raining, but the street is wet: the asphalt glistens artfully beneath the lamp.

"You'll never make a good engineer." What could I say to that?

The fish keeps turning at the same speed; its scales now have a reddish glint.

The sky is still cloudy. There will be more rain. A soldier runs toward the entrance to the park. He stops and looks around. He starts running again. I'm cold. I sit up in bed and pull the blanket over my ears. My left knee hurts. I remain huddled under the blanket, knees bent, face to the wall. Aunt Luiza is walking barefoot in the room next door. The window creaks again. Is the wind making the fish turn around the frame, or is there a hidden mechanism that ... ?

The policeman's daughter must be very tall; she has long thin arms. She never appears at the window beside her father. Nor have I ever seen her leave the house. It's true that I haven't kept watch for hours at a time. I sometimes see her in the morning: she opens the window, takes some deep breaths, strokes her hair down over her shoulder, maybe looking across toward me, or maybe not, closes her window, and disappears. Then the policeman looms up, always with a cap on his head, stout and smiling.

In the next room, Aunt Luiza is pacing lightly over the floor. She'd be better off reading tarot cards. The window creaks under the pressure of the wind. The streetlamp casts a dirty, yellowish light. The fish is probably still turning. I try to glue my knees to my belly. The blood-red window is no longer visible. Yes, there must be a mechanism, however small, however simple! I reach out to feel the rough cold wall. Lower down, near the floor, there are patches of damp.

In Our Backyard

Very early in the morning, Ion would help Mrs. Ignătescu to put the carpets onto the frame in the yard and beat them with a switch or a stick. The dust rose and spread through the yard like mist. The rabbits took fright and scattered, while the chickens withdrew indignantly to their coops at the far end. Mrs. Ignătescu's dogs barked. The racket woke up all the tenants. Mrs. Năstase brought her carpets as well. A window opened, and a shrill voice inside maintained that a pregnant woman needed peace and quiet. This made Mrs. Ignătescu see red: Berta had no husband, but she still thought she could get on her high horse. Ion beat the carpets fiercely and laughed, his face sticky with dust and sweat. The neighbors cursed as they breathed in the dust and sneezed. Mrs. Ignătescu fixed her hands on her hips. Then the milkmaid appeared, hugging her milk canister protectively, as if it were a baby. What a cloud of dust! Old man Căpriță came out of his little room with a bottle; he coughed (demonstratively) until he started to choke. The other tenants also came out to buy some milk. Ion didn't care: he struck the carpets with even more gusto. Mrs. Ignătescu's voice trumpeted above the others. On some occasions, the dustman would arrive at the same time and ring his bell so that everyone knew they could bring their rubbish out; they made a terrible noise as they dragged their bins across the yard. Another quarrel flared up, since Mrs. Ignătescu wasn't going to be the only one to give him a tip. In the end she took her carpets back indoors. Mrs. Năstase only had two, and Ion, now feeling tired, did a superficial job on them. Little by little the din subsided. The chickens crept back, after many a detour, and the rabbits started nibbling again at the slightly rotten wood of the carpet frame. A hen busily led her chicks around, clearing a way for them by striking to left and right with her beak. It was quiet once more: all that could be heard was the cackling of hens and the sizzling of pots and pans in the kitchen. One day Mrs. Năstase also bought a rooster. Mrs. Ignătescu's hens would benefit from it too, but nothing could be done about that. It was a splendid cock! The hens shuddered with pleasure when they first heard its voice and saw its big flame-red crest. As for the rabbits, they were downright servile in the way they welcomed it. It was brought over by a tall, rather strangely dressed young man, who released it in the yard and then, instead of leaving, went timidly up to the carpet frame and began to examine it. Together with his tight-fitting black trousers, like those traditionally worn by peasants, his matching black top gave him the appearance of a gymnast. He had rough fair hair, with a pale oval face. He raised his arm and touched the horizontal bar. He seemed unhappy about something. A bold rabbit prodded his bare foot with its moist, sticky snout. The kid jumped, but looked down and smiled, and stroked the rabbit's gray fur with his heel. Then he stood on tiptoe to see if his head reached the bar, which caused him to bang right into it. He stepped back with a shake of his head and trod on the rabbit, which went scurrying beneath the walnut tree by the fence. Mrs. Ignătescu's voice rang out from somewhere, and the boy ran off. The very next day, though, I saw him prowling around the house and trying to peek through the boards in the fence. Maybe he missed the rooster. In the late evening, he came back with two other boys dressed in the same way and walked into the yard with an air of determination. There they wormed their way over to the carpet frame, and after looking at it for a few moments made some signs to one another. One of them hung onto the bar as in a gym and lifted himself up straight as a candle. The second twisted himself round it like a snake and did a few somersaults. Meanwhile the third stood guard. Silvery in the moonlight, they took turns to frolic on the bar. I never tired of looking at them. What skill, what strength and agility! But their routine ended badly, when the bar began to creak and crackle under the stress and finally broke into pieces. Nothing happened to them; they all landed on their feet like cats, then made a run for it.

When Mrs. Ignătescu discovered the deed, she raised a hue and cry all over the building. She was both indignant and puzzled. Who could have broken the bar? It wasn't just a piece of rope, after all. She took it out on everyone. Where would she beat her carpets now? Although I was questioned too, I kept my mouth shut. I looked understandingly into her protruding eyes but felt overjoyed at this turn of events. I'd be able to sleep longer in the morning from now on. Soon Ion's turn came to be hauled over the coals, but he had no way of knowing anything. May his hand drop off, whoever it was who did it! And, completely unflustered, he picked at his nose with his rough fingers. No need to get so angry, it wasn't such a big deal. He was no joiner himself, of course, but any joiner would immediately know what to do. The rooster tried to climb onto the broken bar, which now hung almost to the ground, but it lost its balance and fell awkwardly among the hens.

I felt calmer for a few days. Nor was I the only one. The hens cackled happily around the carpet frame, hunting for beetles in the rotten wood; the rabbits ran all over the yard, chased by the rooster; and Mrs. Ignătescu's yelping cur got into the habit of watering one leg of the frame.

The gymnasts reappeared one morning. They carried freshly planed planks of wood on their sturdy shoulders, along with axes, hammers, pincers, and a box of nails—as if their task was to erect a scaffold, not to repair an ordinary carpet frame. They had clear blue eyes, and their movements were precise and coordinated as they cheerfully set to work. The whole yard echoed with their hammering. Their solemn labor gave the impression of a dance. Now and then they smiled in mutual understanding, but no words ever passed between them. We soon grew used to them, and no one, not even Mrs. Ignătescu, interfered in any way. The rabbits scurried fearlessly among their bare feet; the hens jumped onto their shoulders and pecked at their food when they took a break under the walnut tree. The days passed, but the work didn't progress much. No one said anything to them, although maybe someone should have. For example, why did they move the legs of the carpet frame closer to each other, and raise them a meter or more higher than before? How would Mrs. Ignătescu's Persian carpet fit on it now? Some stairs would be needed to reach the horizontal bar, once it was in place. What puzzled me most was that Mrs. Ignătescu made no attempt to hurry them. When she came back from the market with a full shopping bag, she stopped and looked at them for a few moments, then went indoors without saying a word. Sometimes Berta came out with her big belly, and as far as I could tell there was a certain attraction in the way she looked at the joiners. Indeed, you might say that everyone not only got used to them but actually took a liking to them. Or anyway that's how it seemed to me; it wouldn't be the first time I was mistaken about such things. The work went slowly. After some time, they seemed to be playing more than working. They performed cartwheels and mid-air somersaults, walked on their hands, and leapfrogged over one another. Or else they had fun teasing the rooster on one of the poles of the carpet frame. For all its pride, it looked more like a painted crow on the end of a stake, without the courage to jump down and only just keeping its balance by spreading its wings. No one said anything to them. I saw Mrs. Năstase pass alongside them, concealing her laughter with a hand to her mouth. Once, when they were away somewhere, I went up to the frame and realized how they had been spending their time. They had driven hundreds of nails into the wretched stakes, until the box they had brought with them on the first day was empty. But soon then they came with another box, and the hammering started again at an even faster pace. They boarded up the legs of the frame from top to bottom. With what skill they drove in the nails! I had to admit it: the kids certainly knew their trade. The heads of the nails were colored in various shades, so that together they formed all kinds of ornamental patterns.

Autumn came. Mrs. Ignătescu, with Ion's help, laid in provisions for the winter, and at the far end of the yard Mrs. Năstase boiled down tomatoes to make a preserved sauce. The rabbits had multiplied on all sides. One evening Berta was taken to the maternity hospital. The joiners went about their business as slowly and meticulously as ever, though with a somewhat greater resolve to finish the job. The day came when they finally fitted the crossbar—a thick, beautifully shiny beam, into which they had driven nails in such a way that it seemed to have black and red painted stripes. The acrobats spun around it, hammering in the last nails. They strengthened it in the corners with diagonal slats. Then, for the first time, the strange thought occurred to me that our carpet frame had become a gallows. It was still rectangular, but stood much taller, and in the end was beautiful to look at. I for one liked it that way; I had no need of a carpet frame. But why didn't Mrs. Ignătescu or Mrs. Năstase protest? However hard I tried, I couldn't make any sense of that. Where would they beat their carpets now? One thing was perfectly clear: only an acrobat with a stepstool could climb up and hang a carpet there. But how would he then beat it? One day, when the milkmaid made a delivery, I asked her what she thought about the transformation: it's a gallows, you see, not a carpet frame any more. She laughed good-naturedly, poured some milk into my jug, and went on her way. Should I tell Mrs. Ignătescu that those charlatans had taken us for a ride? It's true that she didn't know they'd broken the frame in the first place. At the time I'd been as silent as the grave, so was I now going to . . . ? Still, it was really getting to be too much—here in our backyard. Mrs. Ignătescu will really raise hell, I thought with some pleasure. Those kids had better watch out! She'll incite the whole neighborhood against them . . . . The acrobats had just finished decorating the frame with flowers and multicolored streamers. One had a reel of thin cable on his arm—a kind of silk cord. He twirled it around, closing now one eye, now the other. A rabbit nibbled lackadaisically at his heel. I won't tell Mrs. Ignătescu a thing; she can see for herself. It was she who hired them, after all. Now it's too late. Perhaps she wouldn't even believe me and would make me look like the villain of the piece. That kind of thing's happened before. I opened the window to let some cool air in. The sun was setting. The kids took off their jerseys and went to wash at the pump. They were cheerful, more cheerful than ever. They splashed and jostled one another, laughing with their mouths wide open. Their wet bodies glistened with a reddish hue in the sun. Mrs. Ignătescu herself brought them some towels. They gamboled around her, splashing her with water as they chased after one another. Caught up in their playfulness, she began to giggle as if someone was tickling her, and slapped them on the back with her chubby hand. She moved her broad hips jauntily. Mrs. Năstase came out too, together with her husband, Mr. Năstase. Ion picked at his nose and broke into a slanting grin. Everyone was laughing, so very happy. Then the young men suddenly reined themselves in. They became serious rather abruptly. They picked their jerseys clean of dust and wood chips, then put them on again. Mrs. Năstase sent the brood of chickens off to their coop with the help of a stick. The rabbits went home of their own accord, attracted by the cabbage leaves scattered there. Only the rooster stayed behind. The young men made some gestures by way of asking Mrs. Năstase for something. Of course they can, if they've finished their work. They thank her and bow gracefully in unison. Mrs. Ignătescu jauntily goes inside, taking Ion with her, and the two of them come back dragging the large Persian carpet. They young men give her a grateful look. Oh, it's no bother really! They hurry over to help her, and with a few deft but powerful movements spread the carpet out at the foot of the gallows. They look at one another, exchange smiles, and get the performance under way. First they warm up with a few graceful cartwheels and midair somersaults. Then all three at once make an amazing jump onto the crossbar and, as on a trapeze, execute some figures worthy of the greatest acrobats. They twirl round the bar, fluttering like so many wings, throw themselves into the air, hang from one hand, raise themselves up, feet pointing skyward, then drop their heads down and—as everyone holds their breath, dizzy with fear—grip the bar with their feet and remain suspended like bats. After standing stock still for a few moments, Mr. Năstase begins to clap his big hands together. Bravo! Mrs. Ignătescu blots her temples and sweaty brow with a handkerchief. Oof! What a thrill! The young men drop down, still fresh as daisies, and turn to face me. Just then old man Căpriţă appears too, shriveled and hunched over. He's been ill and has a dry cough. The acrobats look toward me. I feel a bit awkward: I'm not sure what they want. The others also stare at me, and Mrs. Ignătescu lets out a contemptuous snort. Fortunately, though, she looks at the young men with such fondness, and they soon start their routines again. This time they dance. The sun sinks ever lower, casting a reddish hue on their cheeks. And how their eyes glimmer! At first there is something stiff and solemn in the way they dance. Grave faces, concentrated expressions. They circle the gallows slowly, coiling elastically round the poles in silence. It's a snake dance. Everyone looks at them excitedly, perhaps even with a little trepidation. Little by little their movements become more vigorous: the somersaults are faster, their faces no longer so serious. Their eyes sparkle more and more. Their arms move almost furiously, their bodies convulse, the dance becomes a frenzy. Faster and faster and faster. Their faces, tinged by the last glimmers of the sun, have something diabolical in them. All that can be heard now is the long-drawn-out hissing of snakes. The boys stop suddenly—right in front of me, very close to the window where I'm stationed. They take a deep bow. Exhausted but happy, hands clinging to their sides, they stare straight at me. They smile in a candid, childlike manner. An indescribable joy blossoms in their eyes. They're so tall, as if they have trickled down from somewhere. They stand straight, right there in front of me, until I can no longer contain the smile of approval for which they have been waiting.

That Circus

The town lay at the foot of a range of hills that grew by stages into proper mountains. By the time the circus set up shop there—it was so long ago—people had cleared some of the forest slopes to build houses. They didn't dare move too far up, although Grandpa prided himself that one of our ancestors, shrugging off the displeasure of his fellow citizens and even the mayor, had put together a kind of cabin right at the top: to live at such heights, far above the town, gazing down on your more or less humble fellow humans—that was too much. He'd been one of a kind, Grandpa boasted, and Mother smiled indulgently. Grandpa had large sinewy hands, and when he spoke his eyes lit up and his fingers danced about like joyful little animals. I was just a kid in those days and couldn't make much sense of things. I knew that in the hills there was a circus with acrobats, conjurors, and huge wild beasts, splendid and terrifying, which were prowling loose or had come down from lairs higher up; no one had the courage to go there anymore, and for a long time the circus people didn't dare go down to town to put on shows, as they'd done in the past. Once in a blue moon a skinny acrobat, wearing a dirty, patched-up sailor's jersey, would go through a few modest routines that even children found unimpressive; or an aging conjuror in a tattered green tail coat would pull some paltry ribbons from his ears or mouth—a snake, a rabbit, no big deal at all. Only old folk still remembered the daylong spectacles that had once set everyone alight with pleasure and awe. There had even been a special place, a kind of arena, where people would gather to behold the wonders:

flying acrobats with fishlike bodies who floated through the air like falcons; rubbery contortionists who scrambled up endless steps until they were lost from sight; dancers and conjurors; and above all the animal trainer I dreamed of so often in childhood. I used to think of him even in later years, although I was sure he was dead and the animals had escaped from their cages or turned wild again, while no one dared to go into the hills and the forest was reclaiming the long-abandoned houses on the slopes. Once upon a time, the trainer would come down from the mountains to the sound of trumpets and, sometimes loud enough to smother them, the growls of wild beasts and the delighted shouts of people waiting at the edge of town. On such days no one went to work and the pealing of church bells shook the towers and roofs; even the mayor, his gray beard strewn over his broad chest, considered it a real holiday, and tail-coated officials appeared on the balcony of the town hall and raised their right arms in a gesture of salute. First came the trumpeters on white and black horses, blowing as loud as they could; then the huge elephant with yellowish tusks and a baldachin covered in gold and precious stones, on which the trainer sat looking absently over the crowd, an ever tauter, ever wearier smile on his desiccated lips; and finally the matchless animals, some loose, some in cages: white giraffes with mauve patches, tigers with red and yellow stripes, bearded lions, large fierce bears of every color looking scornfully at the antlike rush of frightened yet curious spectators, who, eager not to miss a minute of the show that had just begun, could never quite be sure of what was to come, since there was no gong, no spotlight, only a few orange or pink suns made to rise for the great occasion. The trainer remained motionless: his eyes, Grandpa said, bulged sparkling from their sockets, while people awaited the wonders to come with baited breath. And were they ever wonders! Grandpa shouted, as deaf as he was old, but with the trainer's exploits still pristine in his memory. I listened to his tales open-mouthed: it was as if I could see the trainer's long whip rip through the air like a flash of lightning, or the tigers fly above the arena, or the elephants kneel down in prayer, or the white bear climb a rope until it disappeared into the orange sun hovering like a balloon above the audience. Women and children shouted with fear when one of the artistes stuck her curly head into a lion's mouth, then her shoulders and arms, until all you could see were her hips and long legs beating the air as if she were swimming, and then her neck and head again as they came out unharmed; the spectators had fallen silent, but now they were on their feet in the stands, clapping and roaring their approval. Grandpa's lined but agile hands were tigers and ballerinas, bears, dancers, and kangaroos strutting in pursuit of the merrily colored balloons that Plato, the most popular conjuror and the only one allowed to take part in the trainer's act, inflated through a long tube shaped like a shepherd's horn. How happily Grandpa's hands danced on the table as I listened with my mouth slack! Then all of a sudden they would stop and Grandpa's eyes would lose their gleam; it was such a long time ago, after all, and Grandpa was deaf and didn't understand our questions, he fell silent and looked away, his hands lay motionless, still like animals, but animals exhausted by all the futile rushing around. Only he, the old man of the family, had still been able to see circuses, way back in his childhood. And Mother claimed that even that wasn't true, that his stories were based on hearsay or something he'd read somewhere; a good thing he didn't hear her. Anything to do with circuses used to irritate Mother, and I remember how she would torment her tall son when he dressed up like an acrobat, turning red with anger and calling him a dirty little beggar. Everyone else was like her; some do still speak of the circus now and then, but as of something so remote that it's become the stuff of barroom legend, tired banter to be exchanged after a few glasses, and only once all the other topics have been exhausted. Grandpa was one of the last enthusiasts, perhaps the only one I've ever known. After he died, my interest in the circus fell away more and more, probably because all the material about it had been anecdotal. I haven't forgotten Grandpa's stories, but neither do I give them any thought; they lie somewhere deep inside me, surfacing only rarely, when I recall the animal trainer. It's pretty much the same for everyone: a childhood grandfather sits in an armchair, elderly but with nimble hands acting the part of a ballerina or tiger; sometimes his fist—the trainer—clenches and bangs the table, and you're thrilled by his skill and severity; sometimes his hand advances on four finger-paws, fierce but frightened of the trainer's whip, or rises gracefully on the tip of his ring finger and becomes a fearless white ballerina dancing among wild beasts. Yes, Grandpa was an enthusiast: he'd seen all that with his own eyes as a child; he paid no heed to the wry smile on Mother's face. Children believed him and, playing "circus" themselves, invariably wanted to be the trainer—even the girls, who would really have been more suitable as dancers, it would have seemed. When we had a chance, we ran off to the edge of town, where a wall was under construction, and gazed for a long time at the green hills and the yellow, pink, or green patches that we guessed to be circus vehicles abandoned by acrobats and beasts alike after the trainer's death. Few of us ever ventured beyond the walls, and none brought back any new information; some, indeed most, claimed they had seen only forest wildlife common in the area, while others kept a mopey silence, and a few never returned at all, but disappeared climbing the mountains. We cycled near the walls, looking toward the hills and trying to make out wagons, trapeze artists, dancers, animals, even the white elephant covered in gold and precious stones that had carried the famous trainer, the legendary tamer; Grandpa's big knotted fist crashed down on the table, rattling the glasses and making us jump, and we closed our gaping mouths and swallowed hard, our throats parched with emotion. Then we grew up and soon

Grandpa was really old, his fist becoming paler by the day. We got interested in other things. We did still ask him sometimes about the circus dancers, but jokingly and with all manner of innuendo, so that he lost his temper and threatened us with that frail and ancient fist.

When I saw him on his death bed, last breath exhaled, fists clenched across his chest, I remembered all his circus stories and, feeling a little surprised at the anger still visible on his face—it wasn't fear or puzzlement, simply a petrified irritation or even bitterness—I had the brief but potent thought that he had been lying all along. Mother was right: he'd seen nothing yet spoken with such passion, especially when it was a question of the trainer's huge elephant with yellowish tusks, his baldachin decorated with gold and precious stones, his weary smile, and that whole collection of wild animals as splendid as they were frightening. Stretched out there rigid with anger, Grandpa would have liked to keep on lying, even though we no longer had the time to listen to him. Yes, of course, he would have liked to keep on lying . . .

On the Streetcar

I'd been waiting more than a quarter of an hour for the streetcar. Here it was at last! Striking out with elbows and fists, both left and right, I managed to get a foothold on its step and a firm grip on the handrail. A woman in front, the size of a cupboard, was resting on me with all her weight. I followed her through the car, inching my way forward with shoves from shoulders and knee. The tram had started up. The conductor had a suspicious look as she asked for everyone's fare. I smiled sardonically and handed her my carnet of tickets. I must admit it was my lucky day: the fat woman cleared a way for me to the middle of the car, and at the first opportunity I was able to sit down as comfortably as the circumstances allowed. Insensible of the other passengers, I looked out the window at the bustle of the city. Then I grew bored and, shaken by the rattling motion of the streetcar, closed my eyes and began to doze. Or, to be more precise, I fell asleep. When I opened my eyes again, I was surprised that there were no longer any houses or streets to be seen. We had left the city behind. The fields glowed a prodigious blue in the twilight, while the sun created distant shades of red and violet. I could make out some birds flying lower and lower against the gray backdrop of the sky. From somewhere over the horizon appeared a white horse with a flaming mane. The birds pounced on it and struck out with their strong curved beaks. I looked around me. The compartment was empty; not even the conductor was sitting in her place. Through the opposite window I glimpsed the same gleaming plain, like a motionless lake. More frightened horses with fiery manes rushed up to the streetcar, then fell back and away. The huge birds were on the lookout up in the sky. I tugged open the connecting door to speak to the driver, but I couldn't find him either. What a farce: to travel through the countryside without a driver! Soon night would fall and I'd be left alone in this runaway streetcar. I began to miss the fat woman; I'd have felt safer with her there too. I sat on another seat and watched the birds peck at the half-burnt remains of the horses, which in ever greater number were racing toward me desperately, their manes alight, from somewhere over the horizon. A thin cheerful grunting made me turn my head, and at first I felt a stupid fear. A plump pinkish piglet had emerged from under a seat. Why be afraid? Now there are two of us. I took it in my arms and sat again by the window. It was getting dark. The horses with blazing manes galloped beside the tracks, followed relentlessly by the strange birds with beaks of steel. I stroked the piglet, heart in mouth. What fine soft ears it had, and what a velvety mouth! It grunted gently, nestling in my arms. In the end there was still hope. Sooner or later the tracks might come to an end, and then ... the streetcar would head in the other direction, back toward the city.

The Umbrella Shop

I left home beneath a sad, grayish-blue sky. The clouds had stopped passing overhead. There was an oppressive stillness, a heavy sense of foreboding. I felt like running, falling, and banging myself on the ground—crawling on all fours and screaming like a maniac. But I kept myself under control. I walked automatically, with nowhere special in mind, scraping along walls, dragging my shoes on the asphalted pavement. And I gritted my teeth. Then it began to drizzle, with fine silken drops that comforted me as they fell softly onto my cheeks. The rain calmed me down. In shirtsleeves, hands in my trouser pockets, I walked briskly in the rain, without a thought in my head. The sky remained the same: grayish-blue, deathly pale, petrified. The rain became heavier and made me feel cold. I thought of taking shelter somewhere. I went into a passageway, wiped my face, and dried my hair as best I could. I would even have taken off my shirt, but the cold had burrowed inside me.

From a corner of the passage, a dwarf was bleating as he shuffled forward. I took two steps back, but didn't feel scared. It was a strange creature: woman's body plus goat's head, with long blonde hair. Baa! It came even closer, fawning on me and bleating all the time. Unsure how to react, I kept moving back until I found myself outside again in the rain. I took to my heels. I stumbled over a dog, which had darted in front of me from under a gate. I picked myself up and ran on.

Night was closing in. The sky was now an unbearably dark gray. My eyes fell on a sign I had just drawn level with: an umbrella shop. I stopped and went inside, without a moment's hesitation. A strange room, with a dim red light coming from somewhere on one side. There was no one behind the counter. I coughed, to make my presence known, but no one appeared. I looked at the umbrellas lying on racks like birds with folded wings. I sat on one of the padded chairs by the wall and stamped the heels of my shoes in the hope that someone would hear. Finally a velvet curtain parted at the back of the shop. A fat, almost obese woman stepped out, her flesh wrapped in a yellow dressing gown with a pattern of large bright-red flowers. I stood up and made a deep, respectful bow.

"What can I do for you?" A thin, childlike voice.

"You see, er, it started raining and I'm only in my shirtsleeves."

She gave an understanding nod.

"I'd like an umbrella."

"Sure, I'll be glad to help."

She rubbed her fat, ring-studded hands together and smiled at me. She had a large round face, wavy black hair, and a shiny complexion—unnaturally shiny. Red varnished cheekbones, the rest of her face a gleaming yellowish-white, as if made of porcelain. Round, bulbous eyes, like those of a fish.

"I'd like an umbrella . . ."

"Sure, I'll be glad to help."

And she went on smiling at me. Some time passed. She rubbed her fleshy palms together as she smiled, while I, hunching my shoulders, took little steps forward and back and bowed to her ceremoniously. Then she turned slowly, swiveling her large well-padded hips, took an umbrella from the racks, and extended it to me over her shoulder. I opened it and held it above my head. What a beautiful umbrella! Yes, it really was beautiful, with yellow silk tassels attached to an ivory handle in the form of a dragon's head. So why did that sudden sadness come over me? I felt exhausted and wanted to cry—to cry in the lap of that obese, yellow, gleaming woman . . .

"It's too small."

It was as though she had been expecting my reply, because she immediately offered another, larger umbrella. I stood with it in my hand, unopened, and I could tell my eyes were moist. Opposite me, the fat woman had the same smile on her gleaming face.

"This one's also too small."

She calmly handed me another one, which I also rejected, then another and another: dozens of umbrellas, each more beautiful than the last. I could hardly keep from crying, and I was so ashamed that I wanted the earth to swallow me up. But what could I do?

"So, what is it you want?"

"A really big umbrella, for as many people as possible to shelter under. All these are too small . . ."

"Okay, but you're alone."

"Yes, I'm alone."

I put the last umbrella down on the counter.

"But I'd still like a bigger umbrella."

The saleswoman started to put the others back on the racks. She swayed her big heavy hips. I tried hard to smile, looked in vain for an excuse, and respectfully bowed my head almost to the level of the counter. I was more and more embarrassed by my inability to buy anything. More self-abasement, then a sly exit on tiptoe.

It was no longer raining, but the sky was just as gray as before. I dragged my feet over the wet asphalt, passing heedlessly through the puddles that had formed here and there. I walked slowly, without thinking of anything. Close to the walls—water was still trickling from the gutters—always close to the walls. With no aim in mind. The streetlamps came on one after another, although night didn't seem to have fallen yet. They gave off a sad, pale light. The dark leaden sky grew more oppressive as it came lower and lower. A light but cold wind glided over my forehead. I was tired. I walked hesitantly, unsteadily, my arms heavy by my side. I saw her curled up by a fence. When she noticed me, she got up and rushed at me. She was wiggling her thin, bony hips. Baa! She jumped happily around me, shifting from one foot to the other. Jerking her head in every direction, she swiveled back from the waist, swung her hips, and bleated softly. She was dancing! Moved, I stopped and gave her a nod of encouragement. Then, mustering her courage, she took me by the hand—her fingers were cold and rough—and pulled me after her.

Tall and Distinguished

He finished sharpening the pencil—he always left it until last, as it had hard wood and poor-quality lead—then looked at his watch and smiled. The goddamn sharpener! He knocked it against the serrated edge of the ashtray to remove the shavings. It was in the form of an ice skate: that was why he had bought it. He also had a globe, a whale, a nice white elephant, and—why not say?—a ballerina; but they were all useless, with worn-out blades, and the ballerina—forget it. He looked at his watch and smiled. He arranged the files meticulously in his desk drawers and put the stapler in its place, along with the pencil sharpener and the box of paper clips. All he left outside were the green marble pencil box, the inkstand, and a ream of paper—so that there would be something on his desk. Then, finally, he locked it.

It was hot, too hot even. He patted the edges of the radiator. Soon, in the street, it would be freezing; the sudden change in temperature wasn't good, of course. Horşia was reading *Secolul*. He kept the magazine in a half-open drawer and sat there reading it avidly, head sunk between his shoulders, so that all you could see was a tuft of hair. So long as the boss didn't walk in! . . . He rested his elbows on the glass top of his desk and stroked his mustache with a hooked finger; he liked to look distinguished. He drummed his carefully groomed fingernails and considered what the boss would say if he saw Horşia bent like a kid over that drawer. What would he say? Nothing occurred to him— after all, perhaps the boss wouldn't even notice. He took the ice skate from his pocket and, holding it between two fingers, slid it along the ice of his desk; he ran it aground in a heap of snow—the paper ream—then pushed it into making a couple of really fine pirouettes. After a brief hesitation, he bent down, opened a drawer, took out the other pencil sharpeners, and put them on the ice too. But now Horşia was on his feet, jingling his key chain: it was time to go home. He quickly stuffed the whale, the ballerina, and the others into his pocket. Horşia looked at him, squinting slightly: so what, it's your business! He stood up, forgetting to close his sharpener drawer, took his hat from its peg on the rack, put on his new overcoat, and walked through the door ahead of Horşia. He was in no special hurry, but what else could he do? Sometimes that Horşia liked to fool around—in short, he liked to wind him up.

It was no longer snowing. Squashed by so many tires, trampled by so many boots, the snow had taken on the color of halva. It had turned to mud on the tramlines, and had probably disappeared altogether toward the city center, where trucks were rolled out to clear it away. Maybe it'll snow again this evening . . . Leaving the office canteen, he set off homeward by force of habit, but then changed his mind. The sky was overcast, and far away, beyond the trolley cables and telephone wires, it had dark-purple hues. Yellowish-green sparks leaped now and then from the trams; the streetlamps would soon light up—how early darkness fell now! He sauntered along, well protected in his fur gloves—real bear's paws that he held behind his back—and a hat pulled around his ears. The snow was turning a darker shade of gray on the rooftops. He didn't feel cold at all, so he had no reason to enter the cafeteria on the other side of the street. But he crossed all the same. Two thin men and a woman with a pale, birdlike face and ringed eyes were on their way out. After she had gone a few steps down the street, he felt an urge to look at her again; she bore a striking resemblance to Luci. All the streetlamps suddenly went on at the same time, like that evening in the living room after the old white-bearded man had left with an empty bag slung over his red silk shoulders. Then too all the lights had come on at once—in the chandelier and the wall lamps—and shone on the presents piled up beneath the fir tree. Luci, in a bulging dress, first gave him the box with the skates. She knew her stuff, all right! He stood there bemused, supporting himself against the arm of the chair: he didn't have the courage. Nor were there only the skates. He stood with the box in his arms, but Luci insisted that he open it, and the steel blades of the skates were cold and icy-sharp.

He twisted his lips and chewed a corner of his mustache. It seemed to be colder now; there was a tingling behind his eyelids, as if he was about to cry. His ears were beginning to feel stiff, even inside the fur flaps. A tram made an infernal racket. He quickened his steps.

He still had the skates. He didn't put them on for a long time. Luci made fun of his "idyllic love affair," as she put it. He didn't understand, but it was true that he loved the cold steel of the gleaming blades. They also intimidated him: Mr. Tassopol (Tasso, as Luci jokingly called him) suggested that he was afraid of spoiling them, but he didn't say it spitefully, even though he was older than Ştefan . . . He stuck his hands inside the skates and ran them violently over the carpet, cutting its flowers and grass. "You're a skinflint," Ştefan said. "You take after your mother, Luci, in that." That evening Luci quarreled with Ştefan, and he stopped coming around. Only Tasso used to show up; others too, sometimes, but very rarely, and they weren't like Tasso, who let him climb on his knees and tickle his bald patch. Luci used to find that very funny, and said his bald patch was like the mirror that girls inspect on New Year's Eve to catch sight of their intended. In fact, they were all jolly souls, who brought them sweets, chocolate, and toys. But Luci sometimes put her head in her hands and sat staring at a point in the distance. Her eyes would then shrink and become perfectly round: two blue grains, with an evil look in them, darkened by rings, by fear. One day it occurred to him that she was a bird: the sleeves of her kimono hung down like exhausted wings.

He turned on the lights. Complete chaos in his room: unmade bed, duvet half on the floor, a kettle, bread, and salami skin on the table, a crumpled newspaper under a chair, a necktie, the radio playing away. He smiled. He'd been in a hurry that morning and even got to work a few minutes late. He tidied the table, picked up the tie and paper . . . "The 23rd of August Ice Rink is open daily between 10 A.M. and 10 P.M." He undressed quickly and climbed into bed without turning off the light. He didn't feel like reading: his eyes hurt, but for some time he'd been in the habit of going to sleep with the light on. The bulb had no shade, standing bare in its metal holder. And it was a hell of a bulb, with long claws that bored into his skull. If he looked straight at it, the glare sent little golden circles going round and round, picking up speed and fusing together. He turned on his side, pillow over face, and waited for sleep to come: first the steps, steeper than in the apartment block he climbed every day, so many of them, to reach the place where everything is shining and still, in dream. Then he remembered the skates; he saw Luci looking at him like an exhausted bird, and he remembered the skates. Adjustable hinges made it possible to lengthen them as required. "Keep your balance, you're a big boy now," they would say—but it was no good, he still couldn't learn. Sometimes it happened that he'd wake up in the middle of the night, take them out of their box, and smilingly fondle them and stroke their cold, hard blades. Then he'd put them on and, struggling to balance himself, stand lost in admiration in front of the mirror. His feet curved and eventually began to tremble from the tension, but one day he'd have to learn to keep his balance and even glide elegantly around the rink, performing leaps and pirouettes, like this, with one leg bent and arms gracefully outstretched. He'd wear that fine black costume, a bow tie of white silk and a bowler hat. As he went down the steps to the rink, the night sky would be puffy and slightly red, and there would be a little mist. What art he would demonstrate on that mirror surrounded by thousands of spectators, so tall and distinguished as thousands of eyes moist with admiration or envy followed his flight across the ice.

On the Edge of the Sidewalk

When I left home I'd been planning to go to a friend's, but it must have slipped my mind on the way. The sky was gray, like the paving on the streets, or rather like that empty square, as smooth as the round base of a stone jar, which I came to after much wandering; if it hadn't been for the house walls I'd have started running to the edge of the square somewhere on the horizon, running blind, then spinning round faster and faster, climbing the slope of the sky, till I grew dizzy and there was no more up or down. But the house walls were in the way, and the few people out for a stroll or hurrying to an appointment would have stopped me—for humanitarian reasons, of course. So I walked quietly by the roadside, bending my knees a little, keeping my head down so as not to see the sky as gray as the pavement I was treading. I circled the square a couple of times; after all, there's a difference between sky and sidewalk, between leaves and people's shoes crushing them. The asphalt of the sky is smoother, cleaner—or maybe that's an illusion due to distance. I held my hands down by my side, like wing stumps, in order to keep my balance, because I'm so alone and I like to walk on the edge of the sidewalk. And when, rarely, I have to cross the street, I break into a run: not for fear of cars—I like the way they whistle past—but to reach the other sidewalk, the other edge, more quickly. Since I lower my head and hold my arms by my side for the sake of balance, the gray of the sidewalk is exactly the same shade as the gray of the sky—that is, less whitish than usual, with a faintly blue vapor here and there when you look at it closely; sometimes turning pale, like when you think for a moment, without wishing to, that you're going to die. For a moment an eye glistens cheerful and complicit from under a leaf, and then I stop and wait, arms wide open, but it only lasts a moment and perhaps it only seemed like that to me. There's another difference between sky and sidewalk: sometimes the sky appears blue and friendly and you look at it as at a tall, kindly gentleman; you stop, roll your eyes around, and wait for it to stroke you on the head. Then, for just a moment, you think that what is called sky is not the stone trapdoor you know but perhaps a bottomless lake, or the soul of someone on the other side.

I looked up and noticed someone imitating my gestures. I could see he wasn't very tall and had flap ears, and that his arms were open like wings; he was wearing a green overcoat like mine, unfastened and rather on the large side, and was walking on the edge of the sidewalk a few meters ahead. I stopped. So did he. I raised my arm in the direction of the treetop, toward a little break in the clouds. He did the same. Then I crouched down and he crouched down, though he didn't see me; I stretched my arms out in front and to the side and moved them around as in gymnastics; we both lost balance, one foot slipped in the gutter, we fell onto one knee and, after getting up again, broke into a run; much as I tried I couldn't catch him, the distance between us remained the same. I stopped. So did he. We mopped our face and brow with a handkerchief; I saw him panting, his head a little bent, his shoulders rising and falling in time with his breathing. He was tired. And I too was tired. I felt sorry for him. Why was I chasing him like that? People passed by, we were on a busy street, they all looked at me with surprise or contempt, some even stopped for a few moments and shook their head in disapproval. An eye gleamed mockingly from under a leaf in the gutter; I got scared, I felt guilty. Still a few meters in front of me, his head bent in fear or shame, the stubborn man did not move, did not go away. We both looked down at the gray stone of the sidewalk. I felt the slab of sky sink lower and lower to squash us. I again crouched down, my head more and more bent, seeing nothing but asphalt and the gleam of the mocking eye in the gutter. I heard the swishing of car wheels, the pounding of heel plates on the sidewalk, and again I was alone. Then I raised my eyes toward him, got to my feet, and saw him remove the belt from his trousers; he pulled it free as if it were a sword, then bent it and passed one end through the buckle to form a noose—oh my God!—and hurried over to the high black lattice of a front gate. What's he up to—he's not mad, is he? I ran after him, but I stopped to shout for help; a policeman's uniform appeared from round the corner. Help! He wants to kill himself, you've got to stop him; it's all my fault. The policeman ran up, rubber truncheon swinging at his hip; a blue-denimed arm grabbed me round the neck, while a large powerful hand pressed on the vein in my throat. Help! He tore the belt from my hand, shouting: you no-good drunk! And my throat hurt from his rough fist. Then he let go of me. He was looking at the belt in his hand as if it were a snake; his fury and bewilderment had passed. I kept my head down, only occasionally looking up slyly to see what he was doing: he was trying to put on a protective smile, or at least to find a comforting phrase, but he wasn't succeeding; he twirled the belt angrily, but I had no desire to help him. I stepped aside and took to my heels. My dash was so unexpected that, after I had covered a hundred meters, I turned my head and saw him still standing stupefied beside the gate with the tall black lattice; the belt had wound itself like a snake around his hand; he could make no sense of it all. I thumbed my nose at him, then turned back and briskly continued on my way down the sidewalk. My trousers kept falling down, and from time to time I had to pull them back over my hips. One arm was therefore a suspender, only the other a wing, but I was free and the stones on the sidewalk gave off a bluish vapor; the sky was again glowing far away, a bottomless lake or perhaps the soul of someone on the other side.

Icarus

He forgot to switch off the light and fell asleep. He'd slept like that since he was a child: face down, half buried in the pillow, one arm hanging over the edge of the bed, the other beneath his body with the palm turned up; a knee tucked under his belly, resembling a swimmer trapped in a fluid that has suddenly become viscous. The blanket had slipped to one side, the sheet was creased from all his twisting. Now and then he turned his head, shifting his arms and giving relief to a burning cheek, in movements so smooth that if you reduced the pauses between them you'd say they were crawl strokes. There were also moments when he turned on his back, leg bent, mouth slightly open, emitting a faint snore like the buzzing of a bumblebee. But he didn't hold that position for long, probably because the light disturbed him; he then twisted abruptly onto his stomach, the buzzing stopped, and all that could be heard in the room was a deep regular breathing that slightly moistened his pillow.

The blanket was now a heap at the foot of the bed, having been kicked off by a sudden movement. His pajama buttons were open, and his fat white body showed through with a thin covering of long hair. Seeking the coolness of the wall, he abandoned the hot pillow and later tossed it toward a box filled with coals. The shovel propped up against the container fell against the little door of the stove, and the sound roused him from the depths of slumber. His arm rose in the air, pressing against the wall rug that had come three-quarters loose. He rolled over again and, still half-asleep, got up and went to the table. He took a gulp of water from the jug, without bothering to pour it into a glass first. He looked around and, as if remembering something important, went into the bathroom and came back clutching an ironing board. He tried it out across his shoulders, then a little lower at the level of the blades, so that his back was bent forward. His image in the closet mirror looked pretty ridiculous, but that didn't concern him. He removed the suspenders from a pair of pants lying on the back of a chair, and a smile flickered briefly on his lips. But he was in a hurry. With the help of the suspenders, and a ribbon that had once adorned a chocolate egg, he managed to attach the board more or less across his shoulder blades. Then he looked again in the mirror. His striped convict's pajamas and the wooden wings . . . There was nothing funny about it, nothing at all. He moved awkwardly, though, the board wobbling a little on his back, as he went to the window and opened it resolutely. He climbed onto the ledge with some difficulty and looked out.

The city lights floating in the distance held no attraction. The noise of a streetcar jarred on his ears. Fear crept up on him; he hesitated, but only for a moment. He felt the uneven wall under his feet, under his clenched toes, then the fall. Falling, rising, then a smoother descent . . . He kept his head up as much as possible, holding his arms at his side. The board weighed heavily on his shoulder blades. He twisted his whole body to the right, beating his legs, pressed together, like a tail, and steered round the block at the end of the street. Again he swung his legs briefly, like a dolphin, and began to climb. His neck muscles hurt; the beam of a star pierced his eyes. He flew for a long time. The city remained somewhere below, with all its sounds and lights; the air became ever colder and purer. He reached a patch of less dark sky, spread his arms, and saw that they were blue and long. Beside him, the flapping of huge silken wings. An eagle-like butterfly zigzagged around him, closer and closer, touching his face with a cool veil.

Arm darting out, he threw the pillow onto the coal box. The

shovel fell onto the stove, a star exploded way above to the left, and the sound, coming in waves, shook him from the depths of slumber. He raised his arm, pressing it against the florid wall rug that had come loose and fallen over him. He rolled over to the edge of the bed, got up, and went half-asleep to the table. He drank some water from the jug, without bothering to pour it into a glass. He was thirsty. He looked around and, suddenly remembering, hurried into the bathroom and came back with the ironing board. He tried it out across his shoulders, then a little lower at the level of the blades, so that his back was bent forward. The image in the mirror was a little ridiculous, but what could he do? He removed the suspenders from the pants on the back of the chair and gave a weary smile.

Confidences

I met him in the street, quite by chance. I hadn't seen him for a long time, and now he was walking head down in the rain— so there was no need for me to stop. We'd lost touch after he married Olga and went to live in Oneşti. He was walking with his hands in his pockets, eyes on the ground, so I thought he had problems—or else why the hell put on such a performance? He no longer had that brisk gait of old, rolling on the soles of his feet like a high jumper; his shoes now dragged along the sidewalk, his shoulders were pulled up and a little forward. He'd had big plans when he left, and Olga, clinging to his arm, had been happy and in love: she'd have gone anywhere with him. The rain was as fine as on the day they left, but he kept his head bent low and the drops fell coldly on his neck. I'm sure he didn't notice me; I could have just kept going. Yet I grabbed his coat sleeve and stopped him. He looked at me placidly, as if he didn't recognize me. His hand was soft and sticky, like a lump of dough. "How are you, old boy?" I asked, forcing myself to appear as warm and lively as possible. His languor, his indifference, irritated me; the rain kept falling, cold and persistent. "It's been ages since we met!" The overcoat hung loose and creased on his frame, its sleeves threadbare, and the lack of a tie showed off the grime of his shirt collar. Unshaven, with bags under his eyes, he looked like an old man. His eyes lay weary at the back of their sockets. "What's the matter? Are you sick?" He shrugged in annoyance at my questions. Then he led me off to a bar.

I don't like drinking, and some drinks make me feel ill. I

shouldn't have gone with him. The place smelled of alcohol, yeast, something sour, together with ash, sweat, and cigarette stubs ground into the floor. I felt sick: I wanted to get out of there, or at least to be by the window, where I could see the rain fall ever finer and cleaner. "I'm not going any farther inside," I said. He muttered something or other, but he came back and we sat down in front of the window. He ordered a carafe of vodka for two, although I'd already told him I didn't drink. Then he sat there without saying a word, his eyes fixed on the vodka. Maybe he was waiting for me to drink first, angry that I was making such a fuss. "Why aren't you drinking?" I tried to sound gentle and friendly, but my voice wound up sounding dry, almost hostile. "Why aren't you drinking?" I repeated, this time ashamed at sounding both severe and unctuous. And, irritated by his silence, I added: "We came here to drink, right? So why are you sitting there like a mummy? Why don't you drink?" Whereupon I downed a glass of vodka in one gulp. He began to laugh like a man possessed, banging the table with his fist until the carafe toppled over. He was laughing at me, of course, at my contortions and the fit of coughing that had come over me. "Go to hell!" I croaked, the drink burning my throat. I could feel it pass into my stomach and set everything on fire. He called over the waiter and asked for another quarter-liter. There was no more doubt in my mind: he wanted to have some fun at my expense. I got up to leave. "Please don't go! I want to tell you something." His voice was clogged and rasping. I wasn't the least bit curious, but I sat down again—out of politeness or cowardice, call it what you will. The rainy street gleamed through the window, a river growing brighter and brighter through which people trod with shoulders bent.

"Well," he began, "I think you've met my wife Olga." I nodded. I think I met her before you did, you jerk! He downed a large glass of vodka and stared at me, but I looked away. The waiter moved rather like a duck and had a bald patch. There weren't many people in the bar. Someone came in with a dog and sat it down on a chair next to us. What do I care about his wife? I gulped down some more vodka and it seemed to burn less. "No bigger than this, look, like a doll . . . She ended up the size of a doll," he said, gasping, as he leaned over the table and spread out his hands: "No bigger than this!" I didn't want him to continue. We clinked glasses and the waiter waddled over to refill the carafe. The street outside was brighter than ever, although it hadn't stopped raining. The passersby were less huddled up; some children were racing through the water and flapping their arms. I didn't want to hear any more: it didn't interest me and I was even a little afraid. But how could I stop him? He straightened the tablecloth, which was dirty with wine and grease stains, and stared at me full in the face, although I tried my hardest to avoid his eyes. Perhaps I was already blotto. The waiter looked at us stupidly, picking his nose. There were few customers, and each was seated alone at a table. Only the old man had his dog for company. "I'm not lying, really I'm not! No bigger than this!"

He gave me a muddled account, stumbling over every sentence and stopping now and then to drink some more vodka. He'd grabbed my hand, so I had to go on reluctantly listening to him, without understanding much of what he said. His eyes were shining. The waiter brought another flask. "God, what a horror!"

His face was buried in his hands, as if he was crying. But I knew for sure he couldn't be. I pulled away my hand and put it in my pocket. I was sick of it all. "A year ago she was no bigger than a child, do you understand?" What was there to understand? The waiter was probably bored in the absence of customers: he looked over at us, found things to do near our table, brought a plate of mini-gherkins without our asking him. I had no desire to understand. "You know, I saw her just shrink away. And she didn't even realize. She laughed when I told her, she thought I was kidding her. That was a year or so ago." His words came out in a sticky mess.

As he spoke, I looked out at the street, at the children running open-armed beneath the raindrops. He said he hadn't been able to understand either. In particular, he couldn't get her to accept that it was ridiculous for them to go out together to a restaurant or the theater, as she wanted to do. She spent all day playing the piano, and grew sadder all the time without even realizing it. What could he have done? At the factory he was always moody; everyone was walking on eggshells. "Also, after a while, certain things were out of the question, you know what I mean? And I'm still young, after all, still a man. And she got nastier by the day—as well as smaller. God, could she be nasty . . ."

It was no longer raining. A truck stopped in front of the bar, and the driver walked in noisily, slamming the door behind him, as he was used to doing with his vehicle. He was a big man, with a broad back and hair over his forehead; he looked like a bear in his gray fur coat. The waiter shuffled over to take his order. Yes, she was nasty to him, always cursing and complaining that he left her on her own; nights were a torture. He felt sorry for her, but what could he do? "Put yourself in my place." Again he took hold of my hand. "What could I do?" He came home later and later, sometimes not at all. He had an affair with a colleague at work, also an engineer, a clever girl full of the joys of life. Olga got bored alone at home, but what could he do? She wanted to eat out, go to the movies, have some fun . . . But he couldn't have people laughing at him. She was too small.

He stopped talking and asked the waiter for the check.

"Come on, let's go."

"Where to?" My head hurt, and I was sick to death of his story. "Where do you want to go?"

"We're back in town now, you know. There was a scandal, so we packed up and left. What right did they have to interfere? Tell me, what business was it of theirs?"

It was no longer raining; just some water dripping from the eaves. The street glistened like someone with a wet back. Light streamed in from all sides, the clouds were less thick, and people seemed to be floating along.

"Where are we going?"

"To my place. So you can see her."

He lit a cigarette and quickened his pace. I could hardly keep up with him. I'd have liked to wander alone in the streets; my head was as heavy as lead. Why was he telling me all this stuff? To torture me? He knew I'd been in love with her and wanted to get his own back. I took his sleeve and tugged it.

"Stop! I'm not going any farther."

"You can't stop now. You've got to come, I beg you!" He moved his face close to mine, as if he wanted to kiss me, then hissed in my ear: "You must come!"

I couldn't take it any more. I raised my fist and hit him passionately on the cheek. Then I pushed him away and hurried off. I staggered as I ran, looking around me all the while. I stopped by a wall and got some relief by throwing up. When I raised my head, he was there beside me. There was a beseeching, almost humble, look in his eyes.

"You must come. Believe me, you really must. I'm not to blame. Come on!" And he broke into a run, his coattails fluttering in the middle of the street. I ran too and caught up with him. He was panting for breath, his eyes shining. He said in a hoarse whisper: "Believe me, I didn't love that other woman. She was a loudmouth, always tarting herself up, thought she was clever." He took out another cigarette, with trembling fingers. In the end I had to take his lighter and help him. Olga left home one day and vanished for nearly a month. "When she came back she was taller. God, was she taller, and more beautiful! Like she'd been at the start. You won't believe me—no one will." I saw him try to cry and manage only a pathetic whine. "Come on, come and see her! Now she's the Olga from when we started out—my darling Olga."

I couldn't make head or tail of it and felt like throwing up again. He took me timidly by the arm, giving me gentle support. We went off like that toward the station, to where he said he lived. The clouds were breaking up, and more and more patches of blue appeared in the sky. The street wasn't glistening so much; the light had risen higher and spread evenly over the city. He hesitated in front of his door, then stood aside to let me go first.

"Yesterday she grew some more."

"Who?" I asked, confused.

"She grew, do you understand? She's taller than me. And she doesn't love me any more. No more. She spelled it out for me yesterday."

We saw ourselves in the hall mirror: pale, tired, ugly. He began to call her name, going through every room, just like that in his dripping coat and squelching shoes; he even went into the kitchen. There was no one home. There was an unpleasant smell, and I'd have liked to open the window. In the bedroom, the closet doors were wide open and the bed was in complete disorder; a dress lay crumpled on a chair, one sleeve hanging down to the floor. And there was an unpleasant smell.

"She's gone! You see, she's left and won't ever be coming back."

He clung to the back of my coat. His features were distorted, in such a way that I believed he was really suffering and began to sympathize a bit. I took him by the arm and made for us to leave. "She's gone for good! It's all over!"

He went quickly into the next room, then came back. He knelt down to look under the bed, stood on a chair, but no, the suitcase was missing. His hands were covered in dust, large and soft, powerless. I felt a mixture of pity and disgust. I took him by the shoulders and pushed him toward the door. We went into the street. The sky was blue. People were walking with a light step, floating around us—tall.

The Specialist

I live in a quiet area near the edge of town, in a traditional house that's not too cramped but very old. It belongs to a distant relative, who rents a room out to me by the kitchen; it used to be a maid's room and, more recently, was just kept empty. It's small, damp, and full of spiders. But I like it—perhaps because it looks onto a deep garden with plenty of shade. True, the part you can see from my room is more of a walnut grove, since the flowerbeds appear only at the first windows. I forgot to say that the rooms are strung out in a line like railway compartments, which makes the house seem very long. Seen from the street, the garden is a verdant corridor, with flowers up to the middle and real forest at the back. The walls, including the stone one that separates us from the neighbors' yard, are covered with ivy. That's obviously why there's so much damp in my room. Only one thing I find hard to bear: the smell of burnt fat from the kitchen. I always leave the house in the morning while lunch is being prepared, but the smell lingers well into the afternoon, especially in winter when you can't keep the window open for long. A week ago they began preparing for their daughter's big wedding feast. They got a chef to come from a restaurant, and the wood-burning stove never stopped smoking for a couple of days. Cleaver blows, the squeaking meat-grinder, thudding pestle and mortar, sizzling roasts—there was no end to the racket. As for the smells . . . It wouldn't have mattered so much if I'd been able to go out as usual, but unfortunately my shoes were at the cobbler's and no amount of pleading could get him to repair them in less than two days. I sat on my bed with the window wide open—duvet, blanket, and two pillows squeezed tight around my ears. I was choking, stifling in the heat. At nightfall I crept into the garden and came back with an armful of roses and lilies. I hoped their scent would subdue the other odors. I spread them around everywhere: on the bed, over the floor, on the table. I don't know what made me stumble over the suitcase in which I kept my clothes. I lost balance, and only by propping myself against the wall did I manage to stay on my feet. Quite a large piece of plaster fell and shattered, leaving a dark-colored patch behind on the wall. This wasn't too much of an eyesore, because a large part of the damp-eaten wall already looked like the map of an unexplored continent. That evening I didn't pay much attention to it. I swept up the bits of plaster on the floor and went to bed.

The next morning, the preparations for the feast were still at fever pitch. The lady of the house was constantly pestering a girl who was meant to be helping her. The noise they made irritated the specialist in the culinary arts, who said that he couldn't work under such conditions; the time had come to make the cake and he needed to concentrate. He spoke with the authority of a real professional, so the women felt intimidated and stopped talking. My eyes fell on the spot where the new patch had appeared. It was a little above the bedpost—what a strange old-fashioned bed I have!—and it seemed to have grown. In fact, what attracted my attention was something else, hard to explain. I didn't remember exactly what it looked like the previous evening, but it now had a dark-violet hue, visible only at certain moments. The rest of the time it was black and—even stranger—perfectly round. Despite the lilies, a smell of garlic penetrated the room. The voices on the other side became strident again; the mistress wasn't at all pleased with her servant's work. I stretched out wearily on the bed. I really wished I knew what the chef looked like. Such men should be fat, greasy, good-humored—in short, comforting. With some difficulty I raised myself on an elbow to shut the window. In the garden, a light breeze was rustling the walnut leaves. Of course, the *mititei* sausages and the roasts must be cooked just before the meal. "You see, madam," the specialist explained, "the key to good *mititei* is how much you use of each ingredient." To be frank, I like *mititei* too. The chef's full, winning voice made my mouth water. I stuck my nose into the petals of a rose and swallowed hard. Then I finally took the plunge. I opened the kitchen door and signaled to the maid. I must have looked unwell. Pitying me, the mistress asked in a gentle voice whether I'd eaten anything that day. Sure I had. But I'd like the maid to pay a quick call on the cobbler; how much longer am I supposed to stay here in my socks! I slammed the door shut out of pique. To tell the truth, I'd mainly opened it to catch a glimpse of that specialist in the culinary arts, vaguely hoping that the mistress wouldn't be there. But the chef had just then taken a break and gone off somewhere. My eyes fell again on the patch. It now shone more brightly, with a greenish luster. Puzzled, I touched it with my fingertips, then shrugged and climbed into bed. I simply couldn't get to sleep. But I must have been dozing a little when the maid came in. She'd brought me some food, so I could scarcely shout at her for banishing my sleep. I turned over and asked her about the cobbler. Of course, he hadn't even started on my shoes.

"He told me you'll have to be patient. They'll be ready tomorrow."

The maid smelled terribly of sweat. She looked idiotically at the rumpled bed, the filthy bedding, the lifeless flowers on the floor. She didn't see the patch. Or maybe she did but thought nothing of it. Anyway, why was she smiling at me so stupidly? I asked her:

"So where's the chef gone?"

"He went out, but he's back now."

That was all she knew.

"Does he have a mustache?"

She looked at me and laughed. I think she's taken a liking to me. She'd brought me a slice of roast with a green pepper. But she got on my nerves. I sat there in my socks, not knowing what to say. I felt relieved when she left. I looked at the patch again and began to study it closely. Its perfect roundness frightened me. And it was no larger than the lens of a spyglass. A spider came down to its level, then hurried back to the web it had spun in a corner.

Toward evening the rumpus in the kitchen died down. The only sound was of the specialist sharpening his knives. The wedding was scheduled for the next day. Feeling a little better, I threw away the flowers and managed to sleep for two or three hours. My head was clear. A cool, perfumed breath of wind entered from outside. I jumped out of bed and began hunting for my shoes.

Then the specialist came in.

The door opened slowly, with a squeak. The man who appeared in the room was short, thin, and red-haired; he was wearing clothes that were too big for him. He looked at me gravely and, it being quite dark, flicked the light switch to the right of the door, as if he already knew exactly where it was. Something told me it was he, the specialist. But I immediately asked:

"What do you want? Who are you?"

His thick nose glistened beneath the lightbulb. He had a long, lean, bony face; little eyes almost hidden behind the narrow slits of his eyelids. He pointed at the patch and asked me in a professional tone:

"Has that been here a long time?"

I said it had appeared the day before, just as it was getting dark. He took a quick look around. I was a little ashamed of the untidiness in the room, and of the leftover meat I'd dropped on the table. I asked him again who he was. He gave a bored shrug and sat down on the bed. His feet didn't even reach the floor.

"The room's got a lot of damp."

"Yes . . ."

"And what's through there?"

I thought he was talking about the garden.

"No, I meant on the other side of the wall."

"Ah! It's the room where they do the washing. That's why it's so damp."

He smiled, baring toothless gums. He swung his legs—now one, now the other, now both together.

I'd never have thought a specialist would look like that.

Now I understood the maid's contemptuous tone.

"Are you really the specialist?"

No answer. He bent his head to one side, then suddenly said:

"Okay, let's get started."

There was something commanding in the way he'd said it. I jumped out of bed, treading on his little shoes. He took a knife and a scraper out of his pocket. He showed them to me with solemn gestures, then began to examine the patch more attentively. It had a violet sheen again. It was beautiful. He gave me another look and got down to work, muttering something under his breath. First, using the knife, he smoothed the wall all around. Then, holding the scraper in both hands, he began scraping the patch itself. He worked slowly, jaw tightly clenched. I watched his rhythmic movements with admiration from my perch on the bed. Now and again he stopped, took a deep breath, inspected the wall close up as if he was nearsighted, and started to scrape again.

More than an hour passed, without any result. I don't even know what I was expecting to happen. He didn't say a word. Sweat poured off his forehead, and the veins in his temples seemed about to burst. Later in the day, when I was idly looking around, bored and sleepy, he uttered a little cry of triumph. The patch was turning red over a large part of its surface. The specialist ran his hand through his hair and wiped his brow with a handkerchief.

He looked up at me with a start, as if he had only just noticed I was there. Then, as if issuing an order:

"Come and do some yourself!"

I eagerly took the scraper from him and bent over to work on the patch. My movements were faster than his, but it was obvious that I didn't know to scrape properly. The tool gave out high-pitched squeaks, as if I were scraping a sheet of glass. He tried to encourage me:

"Come on, it's always like that at first. Hold it straighter. That's right."

I was putting all my strength into it. The raw-meat red bored through my eye. After another hour, the patch had lost so much of its color that it was a pale pink.

"Let me have it now," he said.

He worked the scraper as precisely and regularly as before. As the patch lost its color, he looked more and more violet. He scraped away happily, even began to whistle. A change took place in me too. I was no longer at all sleepy—in fact, I felt quite excited. I leaned over, looking at him and running my cheek against his russet locks. The patch had taken on a whitish hue. It looked like a windowpane covered with wash. The specialist turned his head to me, eyes gleaming. My heart was racing—but still I couldn't imagine what was about to happen. That screeching of blade on glass, that grinding sound that had previously made me shiver . . . The patch gradually became brighter. The little man's weary hand, veins bulging, kept up the same rhythm. A final screech of the knife, then another cry of joy. The specialist moved sideways and shouted to me:

"Get a look at this!"

I was trembling as I groped my way along the wall like a blind man. I pressed my cheek to it, then my forehead, and finally my eyelids. I couldn't see anything. I was too close, too excited. I swung round, gaping in confusion. The specialist, on the bed, had covered his face with his rough red hands. Maybe he was crying. When he looked at me, his face was flushed, his eyes fixed and staring.

"Did you see?"

He didn't wait for an answer. His voice suddenly weakened, almost to a whisper.

"I don't have the right. I find out where it appeared, I scrape and I scratch, I clean it . . . But I don't have the right."

He ran his hand wearily through his hair. I didn't understand a thing.

"Are you the specialist?"

He nodded, looking at me bitterly. He was so small and sad there, on the edge of the bed.

"Now . . . I must be going."

His steps were hesitant. He picked up his tools and put them in his pocket. He pressed gently on the door handle, looked again at the wall, then swung the door open and disappeared.

After he left, I tried hard to push the bed so that my head would be just below the magic spyglass.

Homesickness

I woke up alone in that creaking bed—do you remember?—a hard bed, where each passing body had added to the balls in the wool-stuffed mattress (if wool it was—there was certainly some kelp too), but that night, or what remained of it, and late into the morning, I slept like a log, and you went away and left me there, in that filthy hotel full of bedbugs—though I didn't feel any that night—you went away and probably ran your hand through my hair as you left, and I stayed behind, there was no other way, the previous evening we had both seen him leave a tall old house near the port and, creeping along the walls, walk down the narrow winding streets that led to the cliff, you grabbed my hand and squeezed it, I put my arm round your shoulder, why are you afraid? no, I'm not afraid, but it's terrible, why is he so nervous, why does he keep to the walls, what answer could I give you? He was dressed in his usual suit, a kind of evening costume with silk lapels, and no doubt he had a chrysanthemum or some other flower in the buttonhole. He dragged his long pointed shoes along the tarmac, walking in a daze without a glance to left or right, as if he had a precise goal and was afraid of arriving late. We followed him for a few hundred meters, then gave up. Yet you continued on your way, you recovered pretty quickly from the shock, you forgot about him.

We couldn't help him anyway.

You're right, we couldn't help him. It would have been best to pretend we'd never seen him.

Never?

Yes, never. Except that I saw him again after you left—even

though I did everything to avoid it; I didn't think about him anymore, I tried to forget he existed. It would have been easier if we'd been together, you and I. But I woke up alone, in that wretched hotel bed; a newspaper was lying thrown in a corner, the very one that announced the circus was leaving town. You should have taken the paper with you.

You'll say I'm a sentimental fool, but I can't help it. Don't think I'm not aware of it—although sentimental isn't the right word. I don't know how to explain.

It doesn't matter, just drop it.

In fact, the announcement appeared in the paper a few days before the circus left. They'd known a long time ahead, since the day it arrived on the ship. People waited impatiently on the quay; it was a clear autumn morning, with a strong, unsettling breeze, and we waited with our hearts in our mouth for them to come ashore. It seems such a long time ago that I'm almost unsure it really happened—the noise in the crowd, that childlike gaiety, the excitement we all felt! . . . What made the strongest impression on local people were the cages with gilded wire netting, from which all kinds of magnificent wild animals looked out with calm dignity, perhaps even a touch of mockery, at the photographers rushing crazily around and waving their cameras. Do you remember?

Well, they already knew they would leave one day: they probably even knew the exact date. Anyway, their boss—that strongly built man always dressed in blue—must have known for sure. Don't you think so?

You see, I don't like—how shall I put it? You don't even need to be here for me to know in advance what you'd reply. I know all your answers. Maybe that's the reason you left. Because you did leave—I'm sure of that. The light falls straight onto the newspaper abandoned there by the chair in the corner.

Let's drop it, eh?

At first I didn't believe it. I figured you'd come back, that you'd gone to watch the sun rise, disgusted with the drunk lying in bed and snoring—I know how that annoys you. I always snore when I've been drinking. I thought you'd come back, so I didn't move from bed. I looked at the newspaper by the chair and thought I'd pretend to be still asleep, so I could see you get wound up. Do you know that you forgot a pair of shoes? In your hurry to get away, you left them there on a chair. I noticed them, and only then did I realize that your suitcase was missing. But I still didn't get out of bed.

And then?

Then I got up. I'll get over it, I said to myself as I got dressed. It was very hot outside. I went back into the room and picked up the newspaper.

You'd have done better to leave it there.

You're right—I said the same to myself afterward. But why didn't you take it with you? You left it on purpose, like you did the shoes. Otherwise I'd have figured you'd gone to watch the sun rise—and I'd have gone back to bed.

You'd have woken up sooner or later. But tell me more . . .

How easy it is for you to be right! Of course I woke up. But I thought you'd gone to watch the sun rise. You'd been wanting to do that for a long time and I hadn't let you; I used to hold you tight in my arms, and if you tried to wriggle free I'd wake up and stop you going. Why do you want to see the sun rise? So you took advantage of my drunken sleep, plus my snoring, and you hit the road. I'd have gone back to bed.

And never woken up?

I know that's what you'll say, what you could say, what you might have said. But you went off and left me in that wretched bed that creaked at the slightest movement—do you remember?— full of woolen balls, or maybe it was kelp, I mean the mattress, how many bodies must have writhed on it, you left me sleeping there like a log. It was terrible. When I woke up, I left the room, then came back and read the paper, then went out again. I felt I was suffocating. I didn't want to think of him anymore: there was no point. I tried to forget and I got drunk the next few days too. When I woke up, I'd see your shoes and the paper left by the chair, and it would begin all over again.

But tell me, did you really see him?

I know the question in your eyes, the surprise that is doubtless feigned, because if you'd just stop and think (though you don't stop, you only go away), if you wanted to be completely sincere, you'd realize that in fact it doesn't interest you. Isn't that splendid! Since it doesn't interest you, you could have made me forget him too. We'd have made love in that disgusting bed full of balls of wool or kelp and teeming with bedbugs; we'd have thrown the newspaper out with the trash and, if necessary, we wouldn't have gone out until he'd made up his mind to fly. But you left. You stroked my hair maternally and left. You'd known for a long time that you'd be leaving—ever since you arrived. It couldn't have been otherwise. The evening before, we both saw him and you seemed more troubled than me. Perhaps you were even . . .

Tell me more, rather.

Tell you what? There's nothing to tell. You forgot your shoes, or maybe you left them on purpose like you did the newspaper. So I left the hotel and just wandered around. I always came back drunk. Like that I escaped the bedbugs: I could no longer feel them. I was sleeping like a log. But, as you said, I'd still have woken up eventually. In the same room. The light raced joyfully over the walls: I noticed the shoes and the newspaper, and I tried to doze off again—maybe you'd gone to watch the sun rise or simply to take a walk—but sleep wouldn't come and I had to get up and go out. To tell the truth, I didn't really miss you. But it would have been easier together—I mean, if we'd stayed together. Perhaps I'd have ended up forgetting. You'd have gotten upset now and then; I'd have held you in my arms, protectively, and the time would have passed more quickly.

Sure, sure, at some point I'd have woken up alone, but later, a little later.

A few days after you left, the sea was no longer so rough: it became calmer, as if by magic. Probably that's what gave him some hope—I don't know. On the other hand, the waves weren't what had been stopping him. It was nearing evening and I was walking on the cliff. Alone. I watched the ebbing waves become smaller and smaller, and as the sun went down on the other side the sea grew pale and a thin but increasingly visible mist spread from the horizon over the increasingly white, liquid expanse; it was like steam, as if the sea was gasping for breath . . .

Oh, please! Tell me what you saw, rather. Is it true that you saw him?

Sure I saw him. But he was standing with his back to me, one hand lightly touching the parapet. And, well, there was even the top hat—although surely other people can wear those too?

Cut the jokes! What top hat are you talking about?

I'm serious! What I mean is that it isn't because of the top hat that I'm sure I saw him. The top hat! I agree, there was a touch of defiance in it, in that ostentatious elegance. But there was also something else, something he could always be recognized by. I'm not from here! I'm not from these parts! Do you understand? That hat of his was a cry, like his wings. Pride and despair at the same time—both ridiculous, both without any point. It's hard for me to explain . . .

So, you saw him? Are you sure about that?

Let's be methodical about this. Why can't you leave me alone? You keep interrupting all the time, even when you're not here beside me, even if you left me in that hotel room full of bedbugs . . .

Cut it out!

Anyway, the sea was calm, the waves had retreated as if under orders. Then the fog started to clear. It was wonderful! You've no idea how sad and wonderful it was! I walked on the cliff, shoulders bent, hands behind my back, and from time to time I moved close to the parapet and ran my hands over the rough stone. Fascinated by the view, I didn't look around me. Besides, the cliff was deserted, more or more deserted. I stood motionless, looking at the thin vapor that joined the sea to a sky of the same grayish-white, and I didn't notice when or from where he appeared.

And it really was him?

I told you, it's not a question of the top hat; it may not even have been a top hat he was wearing. I was quite a long way from him: fifty or sixty meters, maybe more. A lion was lying by his side.

A lion?

Yes. Like we saw together in that picture book. The one you pointed out to me.

As I stood there, resting against the parapet and stroking the warm rough stone, I suddenly felt that I was no longer alone. I turned my head and saw him. His wings were trembling slightly. You could see he was excited. Dressed in his worn black suit, with a flower coquettishly placed in the buttonhole, he was staring toward the horizon. He saw nothing around him. He kept his eyes fixed on the sea and sky, the mist.

He must have wanted to fly!

Yes. He raised himself on tiptoe a few times, ready to take off, but then the lion roared; I could see its curled lips, as if it was laughing. He didn't turn round. He remained stock-still. He had been abandoned here, in some hotel room crawling with bedbugs; he no longer had anything to do and each morning would look at his increasingly dirty wings, the top hat, the newspaper on the floor by the chair, the shoes ... And even if he had tried to fly, even if he had decided to climb onto the parapet, holding his hat in place with one hand and keeping his balance with the other, then stood on tiptoe to head suddenly heavenward with desperately flapping wings, higher and higher, looking like a seagull, swallow, or ladybird, even then, after describing a circle and another and another, each one lower than the last, I'm sure he would have returned, perhaps without the top hat, which would have made him, if not more ridiculous, more insignificant—the top hat had its purpose. Or else it's that I've gotten used to it.

And did he try to fly?

No, he didn't. His wings just quivered.

The Bird

First I saw the wall and that darkish picture: a landscape, a garden, or just a vase of flowers; then, in the middle of the room, the top of a long dining table, with a fruit bowl that was sometimes empty, sometimes filled with oranges and bright-red Jonathan apples; and, finally, on a tall narrow table in a corner, the telephone, extraordinarily large and black. It was like an animal lying in wait, although that isn't the most suitable comparison; in fact, it didn't have anything animal about it, save perhaps that controlled aggression, being so black and cold and mineral. Anyway, the sense that it was watching and waiting was evident, at least to me, who saw it—studied it!—so many times. There wasn't much else to be seen in the room: the backs of two or three chairs, the arm of an armchair, the side of a cupboard or sideboard. That was all.

Then I would focus on the next floor, where the girl sat at a school desk, perching her knees on the side and supporting her back on the chair, thighs completely bared and face shielded from my eyes by a book wrapped in blue paper that she held in both hands. But the book was too close to her nose and eyebrows for me to be fooled; sometimes her eyes appeared as well, as if she were adjusting a visor, and then she covered part of her thigh with one hand, lowered the book more and more with the other, and— when I moved my hand with outstretched fingers at the level of my forehead to attract her attention—slammed the book onto her desk, returned to a normal position, and rested her elbows dutifully on the wood of the desk, attentive, concentrating on the book, occasionally reaching out for a notebook and jotting down a sentence or two with a pencil or fountain pen; I turned my back, took off my pajamas—only the upper part of my body was visible—and started twisting and turning by the window, opening my arms wide and breathing deeply, or raising them above my head on tiptoe, at which point I surprised her staring in my direction, craning her neck like a bird, her forehead almost touching the windowpane, while I flashed a mocking smile and gave her an open-handed wave; she covered her face with the book, perhaps blushing, I couldn't tell, she was tall and pretty, with legs as full and white as her breasts. I drew the curtain and lay on the bed. In the next room Matilda was groaning.

From the bathroom I saw the boy with the violin: lean and lanky, screeching all day in his pajamas, with the window open for hours. The neighbors must have grown used to him, as you grow used to the sound of cars and trams in the street until you no longer even hear them. The boy's mother often walked around in her slip, it's true she was slimmer than Matilda and still quite young; she would sit deep in thought by the window, or perhaps, like me, she was curious about what went on in the house opposite. She had broad hips, which she swayed as she passed from room to room, and large, rather loose, breasts. Her husband appeared less often; he wore a mustache and had large thick hands, I'd like to have seen those slaughterman's or woodcutter's hands fondling her hips, but unfortunately their bedroom was on the street side of the house.

Again someone came to see Matilda. I pulled the pillow around my ears, so I could sleep.

The schoolgirl's father is a captain, or even a colonel, I don't know much about ranks; sometimes he goes into her room and stops in the middle, she's wrapped up in her work and doesn't notice him, he hesitates but finally steels his nerve, tiptoes up to the chair where she sits holding her forehead and gripping a pencil between her teeth, and timidly strokes her hair, happy

that he always finds her deep in a book; only then does she deign
to turn around and cast a glance at him, maybe even a smile,
and then he exits as stealthily as he entered. A large black car
comes to pick him up every day. I've never seen her mother. I'd
wriggle around in my bedding, adjust the pillow beneath my
head, remove it and put it back again, place another over my ear,
pull the bedspread up under my chin, but then I would be too
hot, so I'd throw it to the bottom of the bed and lie flat on my
belly, one knee bent, squashed against the hard mattress and its
strong metal springs. I've never seen her leave the house to go to
school or anywhere. Nor have I ever come across her in the street.
It's true I haven't done anything to make it happen: I haven't lain
in wait for her behind that tree across the street, or on a porch,
or in the front hall of that old house on the corner, nor have I
loitered at the gates of the school where I assume she must go,
I don't even know her name; only once, when I saw her putting
on her uniform, gathering her books from the table, and stuffing
them into her satchel, did I quickly get dressed, run down the
creaking, screeching wooden stairs and stroll around in front of
the house for a few minutes, then cross to the other sidewalk,
whistling and holding my hands behind my back, probably more
funny-looking than suspicious, although a guy I hadn't noticed
before looked at me a few times, first amused, then intrigued,
and finally severe, and winked and pursed his lips, but maybe
that's only how it seemed to me, and he too looked funny, more
funny than suspicious, with a hooked nose—an aquiline nose, he
probably says to comfort himself in front of the mirror—I spat
and moved away, and since then I haven't repeated the scene, it
was too humiliating. I must admit that I'd have liked her to come
to me: to climb the narrow creaking staircase, pause blushing in
front of my front door, then give a couple of short timid rings,
until Matilda, in her pink slip and yellow-broom slippers, hurried
out—she never allows me to open the door—and finally ask in

a tiny, not too faint voice whether I lived there; excuse me, does a gentleman in green pajamas live in your house, a man with a, how shall I say, athlete's body, he does gymnastics every morning by the window, you see, he undresses and I can't help but see his chest ... Matilda sighs, she's always emotional when she speaks to strangers; she covers her breast with her hand and, yes, of course, young lady, he's at home now, in that room there.

The bed creaked horribly beneath Matilda and her nighttime guest. I sweated under the bedspread, twisting from side to side, so as not to hear Matilda's groans and the creaking of her bed, the squeaking springs, the man's grim panting, her sighs of pleasure, all the sounds that passed through the door between our two rooms, I'll have to move out, I can't stand this any longer. I pressed the pillow more firmly around my ears, I must think of something else, something completely different, I buried my face in the pillow: several men carrying a stretcher—or coffin?—on their shoulders head toward a river, the sky is blue, but a thin fog has woven itself around the group. The fog becomes denser and denser, I can no longer see anything, suddenly a door slams, and without meaning to I lifted the pillow from my ears and listened, a little afraid, to the shuffling of bare feet in the corridor, in fact it's ridiculous, I again covered my face with the pillow and smiled, I felt my irritation passing, a sweet torpor came over me and, lo and behold, there is the bird Irina bought at the flea market, that brightly colored screeching bird, nearly every color under the sun but not at all vulgar—strange, rather, perhaps because of its long neck and its small yellow eyes that look right past you. I no longer heard a thing: thick red velvet curtains fall around me; I opened one eye. A reddish light filtered through from somewhere, and the door handle could be heard moving, and I was back in childhood, scared by the sound of crashing furniture, the formless shapes in the corners, the creaking floorboards, the soft felted steps, no, the shuffling of little feet or claws, a muffled cracking, then padded steps, the steps of a bird, maybe a peacock. Sudden breathing next to my ear, then the warm arms of Mother or Irina.

Who is it you're looking for? The visitor had disturbed her at that late hour: I should have gone to open the door, but I was afraid it might be another of her guests; no one ever came to see me. Who are you looking for? Her voice sounded slightly irritated, she was probably in her bare feet on the cement. Who are you looking for?—but if she didn't get an answer why didn't she just slam the door? It was clear that there could be no answer, since the bird could not speak, it was a bird from the flea market, a poor ceramic bird with a horribly long neck, of course Matilda looked it up and down, she was shorter than it was, because the bird had grown, so much time had passed . . . Or maybe it was the girl from the house opposite, or rather Irina, I'd have so much liked to see her just for a few moments, but I couldn't manage it, it wasn't the first time I'd tried and failed, however hard I tried I couldn't reconstitute her face. It wasn't that I'd forgotten her, sometimes I really missed her, but I couldn't manage to see her; at most a fragment or two, an isolated anatomical feature, as if someone had chopped her up and strewn the pieces in all the corners of my memory; I also still saw her blond, shoulder-length hair, but that was more the visualization of an idea, a conventional image, there are so many young women with long blond hair; yes, a conventional image of the admiration I had for her beautiful hair.

The red velvet curtain parted slowly and the bird came into view, tall and slim, with a neck longer than an ostrich's or perhaps even a giraffe's, and, perched on top, a small head with glassy yellow eyes. Matilda, in a low-neck, see-through nightdress, stood with her arms folded across her fleshy breasts and looked in puzzlement at the unexpected visitor; she moved her eyes back and forth between the bird and me, but she was no longer furious, or even angry, her puzzlement had gradually taken on shades of admiration, and after a few minutes' silence I began to feel a little awkward, Matilda stuck her head inside the curtain and called a man's name: Costache or Mihalache, and the man appeared, wearing only a pair of shorts, bandy-legged, scarcely as high as the bird's breast, and stood next to Matilda, covering his mouth with surprise, or maybe yawning from sleep; he too folded his arms across his chest, then looked at the corpulent woman beside him as if she had asked for his opinion or approval about something she was thinking of doing. Matilda put her arm round his shoulder and glued him to her, protectively, maternally. We stayed like that for a long time, without moving or saying a word, the red light was more and more tiring, I closed my eyelids. The bird lowered its head with a swanlike movement toward my bed, I saw its little yellow eyes through my lashes as they bored into me, and I decided to force my lids shut so that I wouldn't see it anymore; somewhere, farther away, the river is turning red with blood and the stretcher-bearers keep on walking, I looked with horror at their shaven heads, their beak-like noses, and the white togas in which they were dressed. I shrieked.

The telephone was in its place, alert and hostile in its stillness. It seemed to be lying in wait for something or demanding an explanation; it was like the eye of a creature from the Great Beyond, cold but watchful, inert but pitiless, registering everything and weighing it up, so that one day . . .

There was a single orange in the fruit bowl. The light was still too dim to make out the picture on the wall. For now all that could be seen was a rectangular stain, a little to the right of the telephone.

Below, the girl was hard at work studying. She wore a blue dressing gown and had switched on the lamp with the long flexible neck. I tried to attract her attention by waving a tie, a newspaper, a shirt, I took off my pajamas in slow sweeping movements, I turned on the light—for nothing. Then, closer to the window, I looked more closely and saw that she was smiling as she continued to look down. Outside it had started to rain. A gray curtain fell between her and me. Maybe she hadn't been smiling. I looked away. The boy with the violin hadn't yet begun his exercises.

Matilda's gentle snoring could be heard from the other side of the door. I didn't feel like doing anything. I looked once more at the girl, then put on my pajamas and climbed into bed. The ceiling was slightly cracked and dirty, only then did I realize how dirty it was; there was a spider web in a corner, though no sign of the spider, it was probably lying in wait inside a crack; but there were no flies, I didn't see a single one. I shut my eyes, and again the group was heading toward the river that loomed black and oily in the distance. Ten paces farther on I spotted the bird: it was motionless, its little yellow eyes directed toward the river . . .

I had never seen anyone speak on that telephone—not once. You'd have said the place was unoccupied, except that, through the window of the next room, which was obviously part of the same apartment, you sometimes saw in the evening the shape of a tall woman combing her hair or simply looking at herself in a wall mirror or disappearing through a door into another room or the bathroom. Only her outline was visible, thick curtains hung at the window, which was never opened. In the room with the telephone, which seemed to be the dining room, there were no curtains but only wooden blinds that were never lowered, or at least I never saw them down. Why should anyone lower them if no one ever went into the room? Perhaps it's because it was never used that the telephone seemed so cruel in its menacing expectation. It's true that I never spied for more than two hours at a time, I'd always lie on the bed, pick up a book, or simply fall asleep. So I can't be sure that no one ever went into the room to speak on the phone, or to potter around in there, arranging the apples or oranges I saw in the fruit bowl, for example, sometimes many, sometimes few, sometimes none at all. Meals must have been eaten in another room, or modestly in the kitchen, or else, on the contrary, at a restaurant: it takes all kinds . . .

My right eye was twitching. I've forgotten if that's a good or bad omen. Anyway Matilda insists it's bad (or good?), and Irina the opposite. That I know for sure.

It was no longer raining. The girl was off at school, of course, she wasn't going to spend all day staring at me. Matilda wasn't home either. I was alone. I stood by the window in my green pajamas, unable to take my eyes off that telephone. As usual, there wasn't much light in the telephone room, the painting was no more than a stain on the gray wall. The sky was filled with thick clouds, which had drifted lower and lower over the roof of the house opposite. The light went on in a room to the side. A fat man in a khaki army uniform leaned out to look into the yard. It was quiet. A very quiet neighborhood. The quietness fascinated me—that's why I rented the little room.

I didn't know what to do . . . I picked up a book, lay on the bed, tried to read. I didn't understand a thing. I felt weighed down somehow, overcome by the heaviness of the air, increasingly dense, increasingly stuffy. The ceiling moved a little lower, making the room seem smaller. I should have gotten up and opened the window: I was choking. Of course, living in an attic, you can't have too many pretensions. Matilda treats me wonderfully, there's nothing I could reproach her with. Every morning she brings me coffee in my room, without knocking first; she thinks that shows how fond she is of me. First I hear a slight bumping sound, then scratching, I see the handle move slowly down under the pressure of a skillful white hand, the door opens a little, and there's Matilda's downy white arm carrying a green plastic tray, on which a cup of coffee sits steaming. Thank you, you're very kind. She doesn't answer. I can guess there's a smile on her chubby round face, but because it's smeared with cream she remains behind the door; only her arm extends into the room, almost unnaturally long as it places the coffee on the table.

The girl didn't come, nor did I see the boy with the violin. The army man turned off his light. It started to rain again—a fine, copious rain. I sat at the table, facing the window as I usually do. The telephone was in its place, motionless, never anywhere else; it's always there, in the corner on the left. It seemed larger than ever, lying with even greater menace in its perpetual wait. I didn't know what to do. I was bored, I didn't feel like doing anything. The girl wasn't at home, there was no sign of the violinist or his mother, and the officer had probably gone out too. I went and knocked on Matilda's door. No answer. I opened it. There was no one in the room: neither she nor Mihalache. They weren't in the kitchen either. I was alone. I went to the window again. Someone entered the telephone room. I couldn't see who, but I felt there was definitely someone there. I strained my eyes. To the right, where only a bit of a sideboard was visible, I glimpsed a figure dressed in such glaring colors that they shone even into the semi-darkness at the back of the room—especially the red and the yellow. Then I saw that a long neck, ending in a small head, rose above the shape. It disappeared into the area I couldn't see from my window, maybe into the bathroom. I waited. My heart thundered for a few minutes, feeling as if it was about to burst. It was the bird, the one from the flea market. I no longer had the slightest doubt. Look, there it is! It's moving there by the sideboard. Visibility was very poor, there was less and less light. Rain continued to fall, stubborn as ever. Clouds gathered ever darker in the sky.

I took off my pajamas and began my gymnastic exercises as usual. I was no longer afraid, just excited. Now I knew. I had to keep calm, avoiding fear or impatience. Now I knew. The bird was walking around, getting closer, will come here one day. Now

I was sure. I sat on the bed, head in hands. There was no longer any point in leaving; no point in setting foot outside of Matilda's. I lay on the bed, face up, legs tight together, hands stiff beside my body. The stretcher slopes down, as if it's slipping from the hands of the bearers. They speed up a little, but choose carefully where to put their feet. The river gleams in the sun, dark and silvery.

The Accident

A droning could be heard in the sky as old Leo said sorry, just a second, and went to the window, one hand holding his razor, the other smeared with lather. He failed to spot the plane and nervously pulled the rather dirty curtains, but the droning went on, where can it be? said Leo, and, sorry, I'll be right back. Mihalache had also stopped work: he raised his scissors to ear level and pretended to tap his forehead a couple of times, as if to say he's crazy; the others laughed at the joke, the droning moved off, becoming less and less audible, and old Leo returned to the shop, puffing and red in the face, I saw it, it was very high . . .

Did you see it, Mister Leo? Yes, I did, and he wiped his hand with a towel, then began to sharpen the razor on the leather strap hanging from the wall. His customer, one cheek shaved, the other still soapy, muttered something or other, and Leo excused himself again and applied some more lather. He then took a couple of steps back, as if to admire his work.

Lică began to speak about aircraft: the French had built a huge one with God knows how many seats, incredibly fast, six or seven hundred miles an hour, I promise you, I'm not making it up . . . No, Mihalache interrupted, it was the Americans, not the French, isn't that right, Mister Leo? But old Leo didn't feel like talking, his mind was elsewhere. He scratched his head with his little fingernail; his hair was turning gray at the temples, and there were a couple of bald patches he had no way of hiding. He looked in the mirror: his mustache was still black, shiny from brilliantine, not yet dyed. It was their problem if they didn't believe it . . .

Been flying this month, Leo? He didn't answer. He had to be careful when he was scraping the razor over someone's throat. How they fidgeted all the time! They asked him things just for the sake of it, because they thought he liked to talk, but the whole shop knew that every month Leo took a day of his annual leave to fly to a distant city, one summer he even got as far as Budapest, in a plane so big you didn't feel you were flying. And each time he'd tell them how the flight had gone, whether there had been air pockets or something wrong with the engine, where it had stopped en route, all kinds of little details, but there had to be a limit, he couldn't spend all day rabbiting on. He washed the customer's face over the sink. Eau de Cologne? Alcohol? Then some fanning with the towel, careful, almost tender strokes of the comb, how young he is, and what a surprising resemblance to the other one! He could see it more clearly now that he was shaved. The young man got up to leave, and old Leo felt himself blush as the guy slipped him a tip.

Mihalache was the only one he sometimes chatted with properly, when they were playing backgammon. He told him that it was best in really small planes, because in the big ones you didn't feel you were flying: you sat in your seat like at the theater, looking out the window at the sky or at clouds as motionless as foam sheep, so that if you couldn't hear the dull sound of the engines you'd think it was all a con, that the plane wasn't moving, what do you mean, not moving? just that, I don't know, like it was hanging from a cable . . . What funny ideas you have! Mihalache said, and he shook the dice in his hands like a crapshooter.

They didn't play in the shop, Mihalache came to his place, he was younger and still a bachelor, you don't know how lucky you are, old Leo said—and he laughed heartily, poured two glasses of *drojdie*,* cheers, then wiped his mouth and mustache with the back of his hand and gave a smack of satisfaction. The dice

* An alcoholic drink made from wine yeast.

left Mihalache's fist and rolled endlessly, okay, you throw them, and Mihalache smiled, right, you're cornered now, you can start reading a paper so you don't get bored, and Leo slapped his knees, poured another glass and downed it in one.

Haven't you ever got dizzy, or felt like throwing up? Old Leo shook the dice in his big red hand—why don't you try it for yourself? The younger man knew Leo would like it if he looked completely taken aback, and maybe he really was. He leaned over the board, one arm raised and his fist still clenched so as not to drop the dice: try what? I'd never climb into one of those chicken coops, if that's what you mean, and the dice rattled merrily. Leo smiled a little haughtily—you're afraid! No, I'm not, but the idea just doesn't grab me. That's what we have trains for, no? Why shouldn't I go by train, where you can look out at fields, mountains, rivers . . . What's the big rush?

Misha had lain down on the flower-patterned bedspread: he was used to the shake, rattle, and roll of the dice, so he was able to sleep soundly. Old Leo, a smile still on his face, continued to play without paying much attention. A car speeded by crazily in the street, a dog began to bark and others followed suit: one hell of a racket. Some ducks quacked with fright in the garden. Old Leo went to the window, then came back. What's up, aren't you playing? He took the dice and threw them onto the polished wooden board. He made a bad move. He slapped his thigh, but you could see he didn't really care. What's up, Leo? Mihalache put his hands on his hips and looked Leo up and down. One of his shirt buttons was missing, his collar was dirty, even the smock he wore at the barber's was none too clean.

Old Leo sharpened his razor and turned his mind elsewhere. He'd been making the same mechanical movements for a good five minutes, as he had done a hundred thousand times before. There was one customer in the shop, who was having his hair cut by Mihalache. It was hot. The driver hadn't stopped, it was past midnight, only a couple of streetlights were on, the others were broken. Old Leo couldn't refrain from shouting a curse, although the car was already out of sight. It was quiet—unusually, preternaturally quiet—not even the dogs were making a sound. A man entered the shop and asked if he was free. Yes, here we are, sit yourself down, then he tested the razor on his thumb, he still had to finish shaving the other customer. You'll drive your razor mad, Lică called out, laughing like an imbecile. Leo didn't answer. The new customer sat in the chair and stretched his legs; he was tired. He looked in the mirror for a few moments: large head with thin reddish hair, round youthful face, many days' spiky growth of beard; then he pressed his neck back against the leather headrest and closed his eyes with a faint sigh. A shave, yes? The young man nodded a few times, dropping his chin onto his chest, and crossed his hands on his belly. The dogs weren't barking, there wasn't a soul in the street, the car had vanished.

Poor old Leo! Mihalache felt sorry for him as he noticed a little round blood stain just beneath his grimy shirt collar. He said nothing and rolled the dice: double six, you're lucky, Leo murmured dreamily, realizing he'd lost another game. The bedcover was worn and frayed by Misha's claws, a whistling snore was now coming from out of his mouth. Your turn, Mihalache said, and Leo took the dice, shook them, and hurled them onto the table; one rolled onto the carpet, Mihalache bent down to pick it up and accidentally knocked his head against the board so that the pieces moved out of place and became mixed up. Mihalache was red in the face from the effort and annoyance, after all, he'd been on the point of winning. I'm not going to play anymore if you don't pay attention! But Leo remained calm, still with a faraway look in his eyes. They began playing again. It was hot and the *drojdie* had made them a little tipsy. Now they both made mistakes, one after another. The car had passed at high speed and disappeared round a corner—or, who knows, maybe it hadn't been a car, what could he have done about it? He looked at Mihalache, at his slightly bulbous nose, what would he have done in my place? The car had been going like the devil, making all the windows shake, and its lights had lit up the whole room. Car lights, for sure.

He had just finished shaving one cheek when he heard the plane. To hell with it! But the droning grew louder and louder and he couldn't stop himself, he said sorry, just a second, bending over the ear of the customer, who seemed asleep, and dashed to the window, one hand holding his razor, the other smeared with lather. The plane wasn't visible. He hesitated for a moment, then pressed on the door handle, went down the three steps, and hurried across the yard, almost losing his slippers in the process, there was no one in the street, the car had turned onto a side road—no sign of it any longer. He noticed a body lying still in the middle of the road. Leo took a few steps in the direction he thought the car had taken, he had seen its headlights shine right into the room and let out a curse. What would Mihalache have done in his place?

Why are you looking at me, it's your move! Come on, you'll win this one. Old Leo was out of sorts—in fact, for some time he hadn't been feeling his usual self . . . Mihalache stopped working too, raised his scissors to ear level and pretended to tap his forehead a few times: the guy's crazy. Lică laughed, and the others did too, a big joke. The droning of the plane grew fainter and old Leo came back, puffing slightly, razor in one hand, lather covering the other, everyone remained silent and looked at him. Did you see it, Leo? Lică asked, because the silence was becoming awkward. Yes, I saw it, and he wiped his hand with a towel, then began to sharpen the razor on the leather strap. They all knew how much old Leo liked planes, but this was a bit much, they thought. What's up, have you stopped playing? And Mihalache rattled the dice in the hollow of his hand.

Leo lived somewhere on the outskirts of town, in a long

low house where he had two rooms and a kitchen, the rest was occupied by other tenants. The backyard was unpaved, and when his wife was alive they grew some flowers there. There was a pump in the back, and next to it an old apricot tree that was beginning to wither. Some ducks waddled around quacking, and a few geese that weren't his gaggled away; maybe they belonged to the other tenants, or maybe to the neighbors, because they passed freely enough through the hole in the fence between the two yards. On Sundays, especially in summer, Mihalache came round and they played backgammon. Mihalache was younger and had incredible luck with the dice, I bet you've loaded them—loaded them? like hell I have, get on with it, it's your turn, do you think it's just a game of chance? Leo took another gulp, straight from the bottle, Mihalache pretended not to notice and rolled the dice, they took a long time to settle, droning like a plane in the sky, way up where it's blue and silent, above those snowy, icy peaks more beautiful than real mountains, or giant sheep as white as foam, or maybe the hair of a graybeard suspended between heaven and earth . . . But haven't you ever felt dizzy? He shook his head and looked at Mihalache with a gentle smile. Why don't you give a try? It's so good to fly through the air, knowing there are countless little ant-like creatures down below, and you're up there and you close your eyes and you have wings. —But I thought you said you hardly feel anything in a plane. —That's true, it's only in small planes that you . . . and even in them. Then Mihalache lost his temper and said he didn't understand: the devil take him if he could see any point in running risks when there are plenty of trains that are cheaper and more practical, and you can look out the window and admire the countryside, the mountains and plains . . . What's the big rush?

He lathered the customer's cheek again . . . Motionless, hands across his belly like a dead man, he seemed to be asleep. Leo shuffled up hesitantly, dragging his slippers along the ground.

He saw that the victim was young, almost a child, and that he had wings—large white wings. He bent over and couldn't see a drop of blood, not the slightest trace. Maybe they'd tossed him from the car after killing him with a blow to the head, or maybe no car had been involved at all, he'd simply crashed down from exhaustion onto the darkened tarmac. Been flying anywhere this month, Mister Leo? He didn't answer. Why do they pester him so, what's their game? Under the chin, near the Adam's apple, the beard was even rougher and sprouting all over. He had to be careful. What would Mihalache have done in his place? Probably not gone into the street, in his shirt and slippers, after midnight, but turned over and gone back to sleep. But he didn't sleep, that's it, he couldn't get to sleep, period. He'd played backgammon with Mihalache all afternoon, and those wretched dice kept buzzing in his ears. He wriggled on the bedsheet, unintentionally kicking Misha, who miaowed and shifted position, though not enough to escape another blow. He couldn't get to sleep. He tried everything: thought of the day he flew for the first time, of the night before takeoff, of his fear that they wouldn't let him on the plane, what are you doing here?—it was a small pleasure aircraft; it's best with small planes, in those big ones you don't feel you're flying, you sit strapped to your seat with a safety-belt (though he mostly forgot to put his on) and look through the window at clouds as motionless as mountains covered with snow and ice, and if you didn't hear the dull noise of the engines . . . And haven't you ever thrown up? No, never dizzy and never nauseous, a born flyer! He smiled. Then Mihalache lost his temper, went red in the face: it makes no sense, it's absurd.

Silence. Only Misha curled at his feet, snoring and purring away beneath the blanket. Then suddenly the noise of engine and wheels racing madly on the cobblestones. He couldn't stop himself; the car's lights—like a plane taking off—lit up the room, then he tossed the blanket aside, Misha miaowed in fear, and he put on his slippers, headed straight for the door, pushed the handle down, and, in a few moments, found himself outside in the street, shouting curses. The car was no longer to be seen. Criminals! Brutes! He went a few steps in the direction he thought the big black car had taken, off to the left, then turned back and saw the white body lying in the road. The wings were long—longer than the arms. He stroked them: a soft white fluff, as on a goose or swan. He looked around but saw no one, bent down, grabbed the young man under the arms, and began to pull him, the wings dangled listless, perhaps he wasn't dead, perhaps he would come back to life. There wasn't a soul in the street, it was silent and smelled of lilies and carnations. A preternatural silence. All that could be heard was his slippers dragging on the paving, then on the ground covered with little tufts of grass, then on the steps, the three steps, and the banging of the handle. The wings wouldn't fit through the doorframe, so he had to turn the body on its side; it wasn't too heavy and felt warm through the thin silk shirt with a large lace collar. Then he became afraid and began to push and shake the body of the winged creature that he was dragging into his home without really knowing why: perhaps he'll pull through, perhaps he's just unconscious . . .

Mihalache folded his arms on his chest and sized Leo up. It wasn't scorn in his eyes—rather concern and a natural curiosity. The dirty collar, the bloodstain, the shirt open at the chest: he was missing a button. Poor old Leo! But he said nothing and threw the dice again. Then it was Leo's turn to throw, but he did it so awkwardly that the dice bounced onto the floor, one rolling under the bed, the other somewhere on the carpet or under the chair. Mihalache bent down to look for them, forget it, Leo said, to hell with them! let's call it a day. He dropped on all fours beside Mihalache, who had stretched out on his belly and was groping under the bed. Forget it, Leo shouted, and the other turned his head, both afraid and puzzled; his fingers touched something soft and fluffy, was that a goose under the bed? Leo grabbed his free arm and began to shake him: leave it be, just leave it there! Mihalache withdrew his other arm and, without saying anything, leaned on the chair and pulled himself up. His hip struck the backgammon box, which had been placed carelessly on a backless kitchen chair; the box toppled over, and the pieces scattered all around the room.

The young man had a large head, reddish hair, and a pale round face. He was handsome, with wings longer than arms that he had used to fly over the city, alone in the harsh air high up in the sky. What could he do? He went to the window: the street was just as quiet and empty as before. For a moment he thought of reporting it to the police, but who would believe him if the man really was dead? They would pester him with all kinds of questions, perhaps give him a beating as well. He took the corpse in his arms and lifted it onto the bed. He stroked the blue velvet pants and the shiny leather shoes with long pointed toes. Perhaps he'll open his eyes . . . He pulled a chair beside the bed and sat thinking for a long time. Something had to be done, that was clear, but what? The young man had thin lips and a pale face, probably he'd broken something when he crashed down onto the road, like a watch falling on cement, and that was the end of that. There was no point reporting it to the police, or shouting for someone to help. What help? He turned the body on its belly, the wings didn't even fit on the bed.

He went panting into the barber's shop, red in the face, his hair tousled—he must have been running. They all looked at him questioningly. Mihalache stopped working too, raised his scissors to ear level and tapped them a few times, as if to say he's crazy; the others laughed, what a joke, and from his corner Lică cackled stupidly: been flying, have you, Mister Leo? Yes, I've been flying, and they roared again: ha! ha! ha! look at Leo circling high above the city, gliding softly like a hawk, like an eagle, and yes, like a lion with big white swan's wings, high up there . . .

Cold

The streetcar was going faster than usual. I was smiling. The speed broke up the forms of houses and people. Other trams glided along in the opposite direction: red, yellow, and blue, so quickly that all I could make out were the colors. The images became long and distorted; maybe they were no longer streetcars. Then, out of the blue, it began to snow. Large flakes fell like pieces of lint, so slowly that they seemed unreal. Honestly, you'd have thought the window was being whitewashed. The city gradually receded into the distance, the houses ever lower, more and more thinly spread. After the last one came an endless iron fence, not very high, and beyond it fog was banked in the shape of monstrous clouds. I had to get off. A few figures were standing there as the streetcar slowed down and stopped. In their long faded blue smocks they looked like shop boys. But they had wings: small, strange, scarcely visible, but definitely wings. Their oblong faces welcoming smiles. Each in turn flapped his little wings. Feeling cold and uneasy, I stuck my hands in my pockets and set out. What was all that bowing about? Although I didn't know the way, I looked straight ahead and speeded up. Not only was it cold, I really did have to hurry. Dusk was becoming a grayish-white shroud. I was almost running alongside the fence. I was cold. For a moment I thought of retracing my steps to find them—perhaps they were coming in the same direction—but I could no longer see anything back there because of the fog. The tarmac road ahead was clear, although unfortunately the restful white light soon took on yellowish hues. I understood when I bumped into a first tall object: I had entered a forest of lampposts. The fog became denser. The posts weren't visible, so I had to grope the cold damp steel with the palms of my hands. Tiredness overcame me. I crouched down at the foot of a streetlight, wrapping my arms around me in an attempt to get warm. Then I stood up and began to jump up and down, slapping myself on my sides and hips. The fog had wrapped me in a shirt of ice; little by little the brutal cold was boring inside me. I blew on my hands like a lunatic. I couldn't run: I'd have risked banging into all the lampposts. "Like a rat in a trap," I shouted out. "A rat!" I scarcely heard my own voice. Someone was throwing cotton wool over me, wrapping me up and stifling me. And the cold! I felt it gnaw at my muscles, just beneath the skin. I felt stiff all over. Threads of fog were entering my lungs. And on top of everything I couldn't forget that I was coming from somewhere.

Through the Keyhole

He was late again. The corridor was empty; he took long strides down it, dragging the soles of his dusty shoes over the cherry-colored carpet. He paused for a few seconds: the tapping sound of a typewriter came from one room, laughter and giggling from another. He was more than a quarter of an hour late, no point in hurrying. Only a few more steps to the door of his own office—a door lower and grayer than the other one, which opened every day and would open now too. For a moment he was tempted to look through the keyhole, but he managed to stop himself: there was no point, Petrache would certainly be there inside, he always was, except on very rare occasions, like when his father was run over by a bus and killed, and he phoned from the hospital in a calm, perhaps slightly husky, voice and said simply that he wouldn't be coming in; only later did they find out what had happened. When he came back, he went as always into their office to check if anyone was late. He's not a bad man—Magda, for example, had been diligently filing her nails and chatting through pursed lips—but he won't stand for carelessness or unpunctuality. That's how he is . . . He won't say anything to him now either, won't give him an earful, just fix those blue, watery eyes on him—such a contrast to his dry, stern face. The latecomer will feel confused and hesitant again, will finally mumble an excuse: the clock, the trolleybus, an accident that blocked the road; Petrache will continue staring at him, without saying a word, then suddenly turn and look out the window at the rooftops of nearby houses due for demolition; a new block is going to be built there.

He pushed the door and went in. First he saw Magda, her rosy knees complete with eyes, mouth, even a nose, and then Valentin. He muttered a good morning, Petrache answered in a metallic voice and looked at the clock. Best to tell him the truth, to spell out what had happened in the nightmarish night, how swords had glistened in flowerpots on the terrace and a winged lion, griffin, or whatever . . . The whole night had been a torment; he was completely drained.

He sat down at his desk, Magda said something, hands wrapped around her cheeks, Valentin let out a laugh, Mr. Petrache looked out the window at the roof tiles across the street. The sky was covered with thin silvery clouds.

Late again! He tried to smile, to gain his indulgence or at least soften the rough lines on his face, the deep furrows between his eyebrows. No success. Petrache turned his head back toward the window.

He opened a drawer, looked for something, failed to find it, and gave up; took a pencil and began to roll it between his fingers; coughed gently a few times. I live a long way away, he said, and there's no bus line and you know how crowded the trolleybus gets . . . He fell silent, coughed again. Magda, as usual, said he was right: those trolleybuses are terrible! She always tried to defend him. He glanced over to thank her with a smile, with a flutter of his eyelids. She was lost in her long red fingernails. She had a round face, a snub nose—ordinary but pleasant enough.

Mr. Petrache cleared his throat but said nothing. Or did he just fail to hear him? After all, he saw him move his lips, so he must have spoken, must have told him off for showing up late again, but his ears had been blocked, he hadn't heard a thing, he'd been floating under water so clear that he could see everyone's faces and habitual actions: Valentin sharpening a pencil with a serious, almost solemn, expression on his face; Magda inspecting her nails, then flapping her hands, moving her head, chattering on and on. But he hadn't heard a thing. He pressed in on his ears quickly a few times: . . . don't let it happen again, Magda looked at him triumphantly, it meant he had been forgiven, he half stood up to thank her, and the next day he was late again.

He was bored at home, had nothing to do, so he went to a movie theater to kill some time. It was a stupid film, or at least that's what it seemed like at first: some guy fell in love with the landlord's daughter—in a house with many rooms, mostly rented out to office workers or individuals with no clear occupation. The guy was given one where all kinds of old stuff lay around in heaps; its only window, thick with dust and three-quarters covered by boxes of jagged cans and bottles, looked into the bathroom. From there he watched how she undressed—a girl of seventeen or eighteen—how she washed, and how she let herself be stroked, kissed, and more by this kid she brought with her to the bathroom, a younger cousin no more than thirteen years old. An insolent little brat! The girl's father collected postage stamps and was probably shacked up with a shop girl who lived right at the top of the building, in the attic. There was an oppressive atmosphere throughout the house; it was filled with corridors, hallways, and assorted nooks and crannies, which looked positively sinister when no one was around; the doors had been white once, but the paint had peeled away and left them looking dirty; their handles were shaped like the heads of animals. Relationships between the tenants were very strange: they hated and spied on one another, suffered from all kinds of obsessions that made them seem even more bizarre, and the whole movie had something obscure and mysterious about it; it was an almost silent film, apart from a few words scattered here and there, a pretty boring film in the end, but it built up tension and left you hanging in the air without any result—what do you mean, no result?—absolutely nothing happened. At one point there was a reel change, and as I didn't have patience to wait for the rest I left the hall, scowled at the usherette despite her stupid smile, and went out to wander the streets. You're lying, Magda said, cheerfully sipping her coffee. What did you say the film was called?

He said no more and returned to his desk. No, he wasn't angry, but what was the point of getting him to talk if she didn't believe what he said? Yes, a cinema on the outskirts of town, somewhere near the old railway station, I'm not sure exactly. I went there because I didn't have anything to do in the evening; I was bored stiff. But no, you can't do things like that! It was like when those cattle were being driven to the slaughterhouse and, all of a sudden, they descended on the tramcar. Haven't you ever seen cattle being driven to the slaughter? Yes, I did once when I was a kid. So why didn't she believe that they stampeded into the tramcar and overturned it, or that some policemen took out their guns and started shooting at the animals? The chaos was indescribable: the poor creatures lost their heads and ran all over the upturned tram; men were screaming, a few women fainted, someone yelled that lions and tigers had escaped from a menagerie and were loose in another street. Which wasn't true.

Well, let's say I believe you . . . What do you mean, let's say? Do you believe me or not? Don't do me any favors, now; I've only got myself to blame if I'm fool enough to tell you these stories. Valentin split his sides laughing, but then he laughs at anything. All I have to do is raise a finger and you crack up: see how stupid you are. Yes, that I am—and he laughed and laughed, clutching his belly. Magda got going too: it was catching.

I don't know if that film really exists, but when I was little I also used to look through the keyhole into my aunt's bedroom. She was as big as a whale, her husband too, both of them acting really, well, weird. Yes, I swear! More peals of laughter followed.

I'd have liked Mr. Petrache to walk in at that point—my own fit of laughter had passed—to walk in and see what state they were in. Magda was in stitches, leaning against the back of her chair, skirt high above her thick bare thighs. Valentin was banging the table with a pencil, his eyes filled with tears. I went over to the connecting door, to look into the next room through a specially bored hole. Don't worry, Magda said, the boss is out at a meeting. It was true: there was no sign of him in his office. A pity!

Tell us about another movie, Magda pleaded, swaying her hips closer to my desk. A film with knights and castles, with life-and-death battles on green fields . . . With that knight who turns into a wolf and eats his mother, Valentin added, delighted with his clever interpolation. I didn't feel like it. There was no point, and to tell the truth I wasn't keen on all the chatter: I had work to do. Best to bury my head in some papers or to think and try remembering which street the house was in—I mean, after I left the cinema . . . Which film did you say you saw? I don't answer. I left, the usherette watched me with a stupid grin on her face, then seemed surprised when I scowled. What did she want? I left and went blindly down a sloping side street with broken paving stones, then into another, thinking of nothing at all, I think that's how it should be, walking without a thought in your head, not looking for anything, no goal in mind, or forgetting that you had one. So, on a little street off to the left (but going where?), then on another one, not knowing how far I've gone, though it couldn't be too far from the cinema. I haven't gone such a long way, but I'm not sure: you can easily go wrong in cases like this.

Magda puts her fleshy hands around his neck, having crept up behind him unnoticed. Come on, out with it! He doesn't move, continuing to say nothing. He didn't go far, and suddenly the house came into view: large iron gates, white gravel paths, flowerpots with swords . . . Are you angry?

He told her he wasn't, scarcely moving his lips. She uncoiled her arms from his neck and stood up straight again, with the usual swaying movement that emphasized her broad hips.

Valentin was smiling—an idiotic smile that was supposed to be ironical. Magda sat at her desk and inspected her nails. She was frowning. What a strange man! Although she'd hinted numerous times that she'd like to go to the movies or to a play with him some afternoon or Sunday, he'd never invited her—and in fact, once, when she had queued up for an hour to buy tickets for them, he had turned her down flat on the pretext of having to visit a sick uncle. Nor did he want to visit her at home: he always left work like a shot, heading to the trolleybus stop, yet he wasn't married and lived alone somewhere on the outskirts of the city; no one had ever been to his place. When do you see all these movies? Magda asked, raising her plump arms above her head in a comical gesture of despair. Valentin started to laugh, but then he furrowed his brow, clammed up, and buried his head in those bulging files.

Come on, she begged, tell us some more. What happened next?

. . . in the end she ran off with a man in a long, bright red car—a tall guy with a mustache and the face of a crook. The girl's father had been an army colonel and was a great stamp collector; he had a strange, three-colored stamp in the form of an equilateral triangle, issued by a former British colony in Africa and showing a native spear flying toward a lion. After his daughter left, the colonel got drunk on whisky every evening and looked at the stamp for hours on end; it seemed to take on a life of its own, and the lion began to run with the spear in its side as if it were a skeletal wing. But at night the kid crept into the room of the china shop salesgirl, nor was he the only one. They climbed the stairs fearfully, or anyway rather mistrustfully, pausing at each step to look left and right. Sometimes in the evening or late at night, but also during the day, they would pass each other like ghosts in the corridor. Everyone spied on everyone else, watching with grave, curious expressions as they went up and down the stairs between the third and fourth floors. And then?

And then, well, the young man who worked as a bank clerk went out one evening for a walk and dropped into a cinema, where he didn't have the patience to stay until the end of the picture; it was a pretty boring movie, in which images kept being repeated obsessively, a kind of collection of gestures, I'm not quite sure how to describe it . . . He lost patience, stood up, and left. On the way out, he had a little contretemps with the usherette, who tried to start a conversation with him—there was something vulgar and repulsive about her, although she wasn't exactly ugly— and he cut her short. He began to wander the streets aimlessly, each one darker and more remote than the last, until he found himself in front of a large iron gate behind which he glimpsed the implausibly white gravel of a path, while on the terrace of the house—or rather villa, since it was very grand, as if money had been no object . . .

He broke off because Mr. Petrache had come into the office, frowning in his usual way. He began to leaf through the papers in a file that he had in front of him. Valentin coughed. Only Magda seemed unperturbed: she took a sandwich from a drawer and began to eat it at a leisurely pace.

There was no point in hurrying: it would no longer make any difference. He looked at his dusty shoes and tried to wipe the toe caps at least on the cherry-colored carpet, which the feet of so many office workers had worn down over the years. He could hear stifled laughter and tapping sounds from the typists' room— the same sounds every morning, the same morning every day, the same day . . . He looked behind him: the corridor was long and empty. He was late, no doubt about that, but he couldn't work out how late: half an hour, an hour, two hours, maybe even more. He didn't stop in front of the door, just pushed the handle down and walked in. Petrache was there, seated before the window: tall and thin, arms folded across his chest. Magda was filing her nails, Valentin was writing in a large, green-covered register; he put his pen down and stared at him. He probably looked terrible: unshaven, eyes red from lack of sleep, tie undone and hanging over his lapel. Magda too looked at him and shook her head, reproachful but also concerned. He dropped his eyes, whispered good morning, and crept over to his desk. He stole a furtive glance at Petrache, who hadn't replied to his greeting and kept his eyes fixed on the window. He took some files from a drawer, then some more from another, put one file back, took another one out, closed the wicket with a bang. Valentin jumped and looked up for a few moments, while Petrache remained silent. He was guilty and had run out of excuses: clock, trolleybus, crowds—any one of them would have sounded ridiculous.

His best course would have been to spill every last detail, or at least to describe the gloomy house—a real villa, with its terrace where swords flashed in the moonbeams, its white gravel paths, its black iron gate—and his escape through the streets, his fear, his lack of courage to switch on the light and look in the mirror. He should tell them as soon as possible, get one step ahead, without waiting for Mr. Petrache to speak—because then he wouldn't be able to interrupt, and the boss was obviously preparing a little speech, look how he's moving his thin, pale lips and swaying slightly, hands in his pockets. It was clear as daylight! He should get a word in first, but how can he tell them, how can I tell them, of the lion that's been flying over the city the last few nights, or of the swords gleaming in the flowerpots? There was only one solution: to say I dreamed it—wasn't I dreaming, in fact?—to say that it was a dream, a nightmare, that I wasn't able to fall asleep all night, that I haven't had a wink of sleep for so many nights. All this was perfectly true, look at the bags under his eyes, red from lack of sleep, look at how he falters and staggers along endless deserted passages, along those white corridors with equally white statues dotted here and there, corridors opening onto dozens of whitewashed rooms with white curtains and white marble floors, where the light comes from long tubes buried high and low in the wall, what's the matter with you? the woman asked tenderly, leaning with her elbows on his desk, what's the matter with you?

He sat there, eyes closed, perhaps asleep, perhaps dreaming, a warm voice whispering in his ear, tell me, are you ill? His leaden eyelids no longer obeyed his commands, fluttering open and shut, in order to see what? Petrache sitting puffed up by the window? Valentin writing diligently, poking out the tip of his tongue, glancing at the boss from time to time out of the corner of his eye? Next to him, Magda's velvety voice pulled him from the endless white labyrinthine corridors, brought him back out into reality—into what everyone, himself included, calls reality. He looked through his eyelashes and saw Petrache half turned from the window, eyebrows frowning terribly, eyes trained on him, everyone was looking at him and waiting, I must tell them, he tried to find his voice, felt a lump forced down his throat, a whitish curtain pulled over his eyelids, so he again finds himself wandering deserted corridors and marble floors, and the neon light, though also white, is milky and wearying. Say, are you ill?

Yes, that was it: ill, seriously ill, and Petrache asked him why he didn't go to the doctor and ask for sick leave, things couldn't go on like this forever. He said "forever" holding his arm perfectly straight in front of him, as in a gymnastics exercise, moving it vigorously from left to right and back again, and it must be clear to everyone that you can't just come to work when you feel like it, there's such a thing as discipline and fixed working hours, no one can do as he pleases . . .

Was he ill? Steel swords are growing instead of plants in the flowerpots, glistening in the moonbeams, and a lion that looks as if it has walked out of a flag or a postage stamp is circling above the house—these were signs one couldn't ignore. I haven't a clue how I found my way here, I went to the movies and found the film boring, monotonous, with the same scenes repeated over and over again as in a nightmare, I got irritated and walked out, the usherette seemed taken aback, she shrugged her shoulders, then gave me a complicit smile with her big red mouth. I left the theater and wandered the streets aimlessly, it felt good, it was a warm, peaceful night, full of fragrances, smelling of lilies and flowering tobacco. Then I saw the black wrought-iron gate twisted in all manner of ornamental flourishes, and I stopped. I'd never seen such a high yet alluring gate. I don't know why, but all that latticework drew your eyes into the front garden, where not a single flower or blade of grass was growing, but white gravel paths gleamed as they wound around gray stone blocks that looked like tombstones, except that they were taller and had no crosses.

Only afterward, when he went in, did he see the swords. He heard the gravel crunch underfoot and he wasn't afraid; of course he was agitated, but you couldn't have said he was afraid.

. . . no one does as he pleases in this country, I thought at least that much was clear to everyone. Petrache's arm chopped the air, first horizontally, from left to right, never the other way round, then vertically, and his words became jerkier, his voice rougher and more forceful.

. . . go on sick leave for a week or two, check yourself into the hospital if necessary. That is, if you're ill. Anyway, I can see you're at least tired—that's obvious, although it's strange to get tired so easily at your age. Valentin stood up and, with a very respectful stare, followed the movements of the boss's arm stretched out like a sword.

He's very tired, it's true. My legs hurt particularly from so many nights running or standing and waiting like a fool, I don't know myself what I wait for. Then I set off again: I go up and down stairs, then up again, that twisted spiral staircase with hundreds and hundreds of steps that get narrower and narrower as you go, so many steps and corridors that lead nowhere, but that's of no importance at all, and anyway you can't be sure, sometimes it seems as if everything has a point, including the endless stairs and the deserted corridors, terrifyingly white and long, all there just to keep you from ever reaching the end of it all (what end?), the huge white door at the end of a final short corridor, or else you imagine you've reached it, after going up and down hundreds and hundreds of steps, panting, sweating, hoping that everything will have an end, although sometimes you realize that what you'd like to call an end is only a pause, a parenthesis: instead of the white spectral corridors, this other corridor with a cherry-colored carpet, on which you drag your dusty feet and stop for a few seconds to listen to the tapping of the typewriters, the laughter and giggling of the typists, and you know you're late (to where?), you're only a few steps away from the door—it'll open for sure—and, before you press on the handle, you're tempted for a few seconds to look through the keyhole, but it's pointless and ludicrous at the same time. Petrache is certainly sitting inside there, no doubt about it at all, his arms folded on his chest in front of the window, and Valentin is writing diligently, Magda filing or admiring her long, polished nails, and she'll speak in your defense, yes, the trolleybus and all those crowds are terrible, and then Petrache leaves (sometimes after a little speech: no one does as he pleases in this country, I thought that much was clear!) and Magda's voice becomes shriller, but also friendlier, are you ill? why did you sit there not saying anything? why didn't you open your mouth? what's the matter with you? tell me, what's the matter? He rolled his pencil between his fingers, forehead down low, admitting his guilt to everyone, and even with her, who always defends him to the boss and worries about him like a fool, he remains silent, not saying a word, not apologizing, not making the slightest attempt to explain himself, however implausibly. He's in no state to do anything but recount the plots of those delirious movies that only he seems to have seen, probably in a dream, that's all he's good for.

He rolled the pencil between his fingers. His eyes were red, the lids swollen, he was obviously ill, but he couldn't find a way of explaining it to Petrache, who wouldn't understand or, worse, would assume he was lying. To wander the streets every night like a madman, to go into people's gardens and houses like a thief, like a sleepwalker. He couldn't sleep (why don't you take a sleeping pill?), and if he did he still dreamed of those places: the iron gate, the gravel and swords, the empty white corridors, the endless stairs he kept going up and down, the brightly lit landing he sometimes reached, from where he turned right into another corridor, much shorter than the rest, with marble walls, and a door at the end that he was unable to open.

My God, how I begged, how I banged, with fists and feet and forehead, and all to no avail: the door remained shut. Nothing could be heard inside, apart from a slight buzzing sound and a long faint ringing that may have existed only in my ears after all that pointless waiting. The door remained shut.

You waited for hours, days, years: in fact, if you think about it, you've been waiting all your life—waiting for the door at the end (or not quite the end!) of the corridor to open, the attic door beyond which is probably nothing, only emptiness, a huge white void. At least that's what could be seen most times when you fell on your knees and looked through the keyhole, your forehead glued to the cold shiny wood. A huge white void—that is, nothing! Only now and then a blue stripe, and beneath it a greenish ribbon that soon disappears, then the white void again, and you wait and wait, Valentin's strident voice, then Magda: are you ill? what's the matter?

How could he explain to them, what could he say? Each time, each morning, as he dragged his feet over the cherry-colored carpet, he thought of telling them—perhaps not all at once, but a few things, little by little. It would have been easier to tell them, his workmates, finding a roundabout way, taking it slowly, until they believed him in the end—or rather understood, he didn't need them to believe him. In fact he tried it: Magda leaning with her elbows on his desk, showing her breasts through the opening in her blouse; Valentin holding the end of his pen between his teeth; both listening attentively. Go on, tell us some more! Magda may have guessed, feeling instinctively that he needed to tell them about the movie he had or hadn't seen, to describe those imaginary scenes (whether imagined by him or someone else) that became jumbled in his head, and eventually, however hard he tried, in their heads as well. Go on from where you left off! They smiled in disbelief, but they liked to listen to him, both attentive and curious, until they got tired and bored or Petrache came into the office.

. . . he glimpsed the swords after he went in. He heard the gravel crunch beneath his feet and he wasn't afraid; agitated, yes, but not afraid.

But why did he go in? Magda asked severely. Who made him go in? I don't know, he mumbled, and he looked over at Valentin, who sat resting his head against the cupboard behind his desk. I don't know, the gravel was gleaming seductively, the lion was still flying above the house, and then, it was probably then that he felt compelled to go in. But who compelled him? Magda was now sitting on his desk, on top of the files. Valentin laughed: what do you mean who? the film director. And he roared as loudly as he could—that is, falsely—much too happy with his joke, much too keen for the others to notice it. Magda paid him no attention, didn't even look at him. She was now lying across his desk, propped up on one elbow. The gate was unlocked: it wasn't even necessary to push it or to press on the handle. I don't know how he found himself on the other side, in the garden, the gravel crunching beneath his feet, but he wasn't afraid. He seemed to feel lighter.

Then he saw the swords. They were glistening in the moonbeams, cold and merciless, and somewhere up above, no longer visible, must have been the lion or griffin or whatever it was. He weaved his way around the gray tombstones and climbed the few steps at the entrance. In fact there were two entrances: he went in by the larger one, the main entrance. Maybe it was a mistake, maybe the two entrances didn't connect with each other.

He hurried inside the villa, because he was now—only now—beginning to feel afraid; the gate seemed to have closed behind him, he couldn't go back, had nowhere to go back to. It was too late . . .

He could see two or three statues at the rear of the entrance hall; they weren't such a shiny white, as there was less light there. A marble staircase with a very broad base appeared before him, twisting up in a spiral that got narrower and narrower, although the stairs themselves became (or seemed to become?) taller. He went up for a long time, until he reached a landing. The staircase continued from there, but it was dangerously narrow: there were no banisters and the void yawning to his left and right terrified him, so he stopped. He felt a little disoriented and looked around him: everything was either a dazzling or a milky white; a passageway opened before him and he started down it with short, hesitant steps; he caught sight of a statue at the end, a lion embracing a swan, went up to it timidly but did not touch it; it seemed to be a plaster figure, cracked here and there, but the pedestal was made of marble, with barely visible little veins in the same bluish color as the corridor walls. Then came a door with a white enamel handle: I hesitated in front of it for a long time before I decided to turn it, first counterclockwise, wrongly, then clockwise; the door gave way, and I pushed some more and entered a white, fairly smallish, empty room; I turned a few times, feeling disoriented, and stumbled like a blind man in the milky darkness until I finally found another door. This led into another room, where a statue of a griffin stood right in the middle, on a white marble floor with little bluish veins like those in the pedestals supporting all the statues in all the blindingly white rooms, where everything was frozen and immobile except for the transparent voile curtains, which I pulled in order to look out the window, although on the other side there were only more white rooms or corridors, in which I sometimes saw the cheap plaster head of a lion.

Having climbed a narrower staircase with much taller steps, I came to another corridor and went into one room and then another, passed into the corridor again, a plaster griffin or lion embracing a swan, then into another corridor on the left, an enamel door handle, which I turned, then into and out of a room, another corridor, a bedroom, another corridor, walking faster and faster, up and down stairs, passing into dozens and dozens of rooms, corridors, hallways, the same or others, hundreds of stairs, and that landing, lit more brightly than before (or is it my imagination?), I turned right into a corridor narrower than the others (or is it my imagination?), broke into a run, it was deserted, no statues, but at the end was a tall door, also white, its handle shaped like a lion's head with gaping mouth. Taking the lion's head in both hands, I turned it as hard as I could, clockwise and counterclockwise, the door didn't open, I tried again, clenching my teeth and using even more force than before, no effect, I banged on the door with my fists and feet, still it didn't open, or even vibrate from the blows, I again took the lion's head in my hands and twisted in both directions, I struggled with it, but it was too strong for me, the door didn't open, I hit it with my palms, fists, knees, shoes, striking desperately until my forehead was covered with sweat from all the effort and all the running down endless corridors, and the door didn't open, remained immobile, grave and unyielding.

Then I collapsed, exhausted, sliding along the door onto my

knees. I remained like that for a long time, arms hanging from the lion's enamel head, until I discovered the keyhole and glued one eye to it (what was I expecting?), and all I saw was a gray, milky whiteness, probably another room that someone kept locked for some reason. There was nothing to be done, so I got to my feet and started off again down the deserted corridors, here and there a plaster statue representing the same animals in various attitudes, I walked blindly (forward, backward?), and because my eyes hurt from all the white I tried keeping them closed and sometimes lost my balance, I pressed my hands and forehead against cold walls of plastered brick or even marble, and remained motionless for a while before moving on. At one point I saw cherry-colored carpet instead of white stone beneath my feet, and then I realize that I'm late again, stop to listen to the tapping of typewriters, the laughter of the typists, then take another ten steps, press down on the handle, and the door opens.

But it's only a pause, a parenthesis, or how shall I put it? Perhaps it's all a dream in which colors and human faces keep appearing, a dream that soon passes because it's made up of scenes that keep repeating themselves, always monotonously alike, and evening comes and I get bored and afraid, I leave home in search of a movie with some other scenes, new or old, in color or black and white; the usherette is always surprised by the face I make, but then she takes pity on me or perhaps just understands much more than others do, giving me a complicit smile with her red, vulgar face; and I go in and out of the movie theater, wander the streets aimlessly, always wanting new ones to appear, like the houses and yards into which I boldly venture; some have little flower beds with petunias, flowering tobacco, or irises, on which I lie down hoping that the night will pass more quickly or, if possible, that I might fall asleep; but I know there's no escape: the iron gate, black and majestic, rises up before me and it's enough for me to stop a moment to find myself again on gravel paths, among gray tombstones that I weave around in a stupid fear; the swords glisten in the moonbeams, and then I go inside, cross the entrance hall, and begin hesitantly, though with the same automatic gestures, to walk up the white marble staircase, looking furtively toward the statues left there in shadowy corners, up and up, feeling the stairs become narrower and higher, until I reach the landing, sometimes not stopping there, but it makes no difference, because later I'll have to come back down, the staircase is getting darker and narrower, and it suddenly ends in complete darkness, my head knocks against something hard—the ceiling? I make my way back, dazed by the white void yawning beside the staircase, come to the landing, the first corridor (or the same one?), then another, go into one room, a second room, corridor, room, room, corridor, until finally I recognize the door and its lion's head that serves as a handle.

A huge white void ... Yet, from time to time, a blue stripe, a clear bright ribbon with another greenish one beneath it, compensates my eyes for all the exhausting whiteness. And I remain there on my knees, even though my steps meanwhile quicken on the cherry-colored carpet, moving toward a room with human faces and gestures of tenderness or rejection, where they sometimes speak, that is, lie, about films they've never seen. I wait, but not for the door to open: I now know it won't open, I've become more modest in my expectations. I wait, patiently watching for those blue stripes and green ribbons, the sky and the fields out there, which only shine for a moment, and only if you remain kneeling, your forehead glued to the cold white wood of the last door.

Waiting

It has been raining nonstop for days—fine raindrops pelting down, with no end in sight. The clouds are still closely packed, neither very high nor very low, as if there's only one of them, a huge grayish-white belly; it's raining, and the oak tree to the right of the shed is bloated with water, its leaves motionless and as heavy as lead. When the freight train passed at dawn, scarcely able to move through the liquid air, the engineer forced a smile and made a vague gesture with his hand—it's the Flood! He, though, didn't respond to the smile: there was no way you could be sure whether it expressed sympathy or sarcasm, or a mixture of the two; he didn't smile back but stood there huddled in his waterproof coat, holding the soaked flag in his left hand, and burying the other in his pocket. Instead of his customary salute, he merely raised the red flag, tattered and rain-soaked, and waved the train on its way half a minute ahead of time—what did it matter? He noticed that old Manolache had come out onto the porch of the freight shed, the former freight shed, an old overcoat around his shoulders—he was cold and probably feeling sick again—the train headed off, creaking at every joint, and the rain continued to fall then as fast as it's falling now. He looks out the window; it seems to have brightened up a little.

He got up from his chair, took the red cap from where it was lying on the birdcage and put it on his head, opened the door, which gave out a creaking sound, and walked down the staircase. The evening before, Luca had been willing to bet that the rain would stop. They'd been playing cards—all three of them—as they did every evening, and Luca had been all cheery: he was winning. You can think that if you like, old Manolache said bearishly, and the boss said, come on, play, there's nothing we can do about it anyway. Nothing we can do about, Luca mumbled, no, nothing, Manolache echoed as he slapped his last card down on the table, I beg your pardon, I won this round!

He went into Luca's office and sat on a rickety old chair; one of its legs was loose and wobbly, like the backrest. Luca was dozing, his head on the desk, but he started, turned toward the man with the mustache and the red, cherry-colored stationmaster's hat, and began to rattle out his piece in a single breath. Nothing before noon, a freight train that'll speed through without stopping, then the express at its usual time; that's all we've been told to expect. Careful you don't fall, he said in a different tone, that chair's had it. The stationmaster stood up and approached Luca's chair; there wasn't another one in that dirty, unswept, dust-filled room. He leaned on the back of the chair. Luca made as if to stand up. Don't worry, stay where you are. The stopping train's probably late, the stationmaster said. I don't know, they haven't said anything about it yet. They both fell silent, perhaps with the same thought in their minds. Anyway, when the stationmaster asked (as he had many times before) why the hell they'd cut out that local train, Luca said nothing and shrugged. The question wasn't meant to be answered: they'd been asking it of each other for the last six months, at first in genuine puzzlement; it had been the only passenger train that still stopped at their station, more out of habit than anything else. They'd been through all the possible theories, all the possible explanations. When they first heard that it had been withdrawn, they angrily began to draft a memorandum many pages long; they spent a whole week on it and ended up arguing with each other over the goddamn wording. Luca insisted on beefing up certain formulations, sometimes in quite violent terms: "we think it is completely arbitrary that," or "you might just as well rip up all the rails." All the rails? the boss laughed. Yes, all of them, so not a single one is left. The stationmaster rose from the table and began to pace up and down the room. It was impossible to write the memorandum in the way the young clerk wanted—he was just out of school, still wet behind the ears. Besides, cutting the train wasn't just some inane idea they'd come up with out of the blue. That accident had played some role . . . Eh, what's the connection? Luca erupted. The freight train derailed because of the snow, and the local train wasn't due for another three hours. Haven't there been other accidents on the line? There was one other, the boss said, a long time ago, when I was working at a different station.

The stationmaster turned around and went to the window. Luca followed him. It was still raining, the forest looked dark and lifeless. Where can it be now, in this rain? He had whispered the question, moving his lips close to the lightly steaming pane of glass. Luca dropped his head and scratched one of the floorboards with his metal toe cap. In the forest? Maybe it's found somewhere it can shelter out there? And the young man returned to his desk, where the telegraph equipment was installed, and began to tap something.

They had an almighty row that day, and Luca wanted to quit his job. He wasn't in the right, though. He flew off the handle and couldn't see sense anymore, isn't that so, Manolache? The old man shrugged or bent his shoulders, wringing his hands at the same time: what could he do about it? The truth was that, since it had become easier to reach the sanatorium from the other side, no one ever got off at their stop any more; the path was overgrown here, and all kinds of animals were prowling around. Yes, all they ever saw was an occasional hunter, or some loony with a backpack who didn't bother to stop and ask them the way before disappearing into the forest. Luca had stormed out and slammed the door. That's no way to behave, Manolache had said, shaking his head, and for three days the only words that the boss and the clerk exchanged with each other had to do with the train timetable. Then they made peace, and all three got drunk and ended up singing and dancing—you can't imagine the scene. When they heard a train would be passing, the boss struggled to button up his blue jacket, took the flag from the neck of a rum bottle they had recently emptied, and went out onto the platform. Look at him tottering, Luca said cheerily from behind the window, he's got to use the flag to stop himself falling. Manolache drank his glass straight down and hiccoughed: lucky that one just flashes through; no one will even give him a glance. Then the stationmaster came back inside.

Manolache entered too, his tatty old coat dripping water. You can hear the wolves howling like in winter, he said, and he sat on the wretched chair that was now pulled up against the wall. No one said another word: Luca stroked a lever with the palm of his hand, while the boss tugged and twirled his mustache; all three were lost in thought. It went on raining outside.

In the end they didn't send a memorandum: there seemed no point. Perhaps no one would even have bothered to read it, or if some four-eyed bureaucrat had seen it and passed it up higher a lot more time would have passed and still nothing would have been done. Luca too was in agreement. They bought an almost new pack of Hungarian cards from a freight train engineer—theirs had been in tatters by then—and played from morning till night. You shouldn't have let it go, Manolache said, shuffling the cards, do you hear? you shouldn't have let it go. It was a big mistake . . . The stationmaster didn't answer and then Luca said halfheartedly: where were we supposed to keep it? it didn't fit in the cage anymore. Come on, play, the boss mumbled, and it was another two or three days before he said: we had to let it go, it had gotten too big . . . I'm telling you, you shouldn't have let it go, Manolache insisted.

What time's the express due? the strong man with the

mustache asked. Luca didn't answer, and the man didn't ask again. They probably haven't sent word about it yet, and Manolache said: so, shall we start playing? but they could see he didn't really feel like it. I've got a pain here, he said, pointing to the left lapel of his overcoat. Why don't you take that wet coat off, the stationmaster said. I had a bad dream last night, the old man said. No one asked him what he had dreamed, the stationmaster stood up and went to the window; the clouds didn't look as thick as before. Manolache sighed: he'd dreamed that he was at the circus and was removing his costume after a training session. Only two spotlights were still on, up near the cheap seats on the left. He saw a lion appear there, grinning like a man and ambling toward him. It stared at him with yellow, perfectly round eyes. He and the lion were alone in the ring. He looked up but, instead of the marquee, he saw the starry sky far away, right up above, or down below, and he became dizzy; the circus span round and round, and he felt that he was slipping over the rim of a well, having leaned too far over the side, and that the lion was falling too, or perhaps flying, on top of his body as he sank into the sky as into water . . .

The clouds were indeed less closely packed, and a rosy light glowed in a patch of sky above the forest. He gripped the window ledge and waited. All that could be heard in the room was the monotonous, exasperating patter of fine raindrops, and the breathing of the other two men. Manolache, bent over the chair, was almost panting. Luca swiveled round and looked toward the window, trying to see over those broad solid shoulders: the sky seemed to be brightening. Come over here a minute, the stationmaster said. Manolache jumped, as if he'd been asleep. Luca stood up and went to the window; the old man joined them a little later. The stationmaster took the clerk by the arm: look, there, above the forest. Yes, Luca mumbled, that means it will soon be heading off. Out there I don't even think it's raining.

That morning it began to snow again. Manolache, wearing

no more than a gray pullover and a high tapering fur hat pulled over his ears, swept the snow from the platform and the side of the track, adding it to the huge heap more than chest-high that had built up on the other side over the past few days. The stationmaster appeared at the window of his upstairs room with lather all over his face, good morning, Manolache, he called out, waving the razor in one hand. Manolache looked up toward the window; the hat was covering his eyes, so he tried to push it back on his head, but he stumbled on the rail (or perhaps on the spade that had slipped between his legs) and fell on his back in the snow. The stationmaster roared with laughter at the window; he was only in shirtsleeves, but he didn't mind the cold—you call this cold?—the sun had cleared a space for itself among the clouds, what a wonderful morning! Then suddenly Luca was there, coming out of his office and shouting something; Manolache still hadn't stood up, he felt so good lying in the snow, what's that? the boss said, I can't hear a thing, and he laughed again, the old man finally got to his feet, supporting himself on the spade handle, the 4223 has derailed, Luca's voice rang out, and this time the man at the window heard the news, leaning over the ledge with the razor in his free hand. The freight train's derailed, Luca shouted, the express will stop here until we get instructions. What's that, it's derailed? I'll be down in a second, the stationmaster said, let me just put my jacket on, and he wiped away the lather, leaving one cheek unshaven. Manolache stuck the spade in the heap of snow and went after Luca into the Traffic Control Office. The young man worked away at the telegraph, which was crackling and whistling like hell, what's it saying? is there more news? Then the stationmaster came in, with a strangely serious expression; you could see he hadn't finished shaving, and there was still some lather under his ear. He came in and slammed the door. He had the red cap on his head, and his jacket was unbuttoned.

I bet tomorrow will be sunny, Luca said as he dealt the cards.

No one answered. Don't you think so? And he sat still, the rest of the cards in his hand, stared at the other two with a look of surprise or inquiry, and repeated: it'll be sunny tomorrow. Come on, forget your theories and deal, the boss said, and Manolache mumbled something about his rheumatism and how it boded no good. This time your rheumatism's got it wrong—or maybe not, maybe it's just that the weather's changing; it's getting better, the sun will come out, and that's why your bones are aching. Come on, get on with the game, the boss said, there's nothing we can do about it anyway. Nothing depends on us, Luca muttered, and that roused Manolache too a little; nothing, he said with evident satisfaction, throwing a card on top of the pile in the middle of the table, nothing.

And now, by the window, Luca could have said: you see I was right, it's stopped raining over the forest, and soon it'll be like that here. The stationmaster had taken him by the arm, emotional as always: look over there, above the forest! The sky had taken on a rosy hue, as if mirroring a little fire, or a tall pyre in the forest. That was the sign. It's obviously not raining anymore, he whispered through his mustache, holding the young man's arm in a clawlike grip. The sky grew redder, and a silvery gray eagle flew up among the forest trees, rising in a spiral as narrow as a screw, sundering the rose and crimson of the sky. How big it's grown! Manolache exclaimed in awe, holding his hand to his mouth. Yes, it's still growing, the *moustachu* said between his teeth. The eagle became smaller and smaller, circling high above in the sky, watching over the wooded hills and the railroad that snaked its way between them. It was a long time since it had really spread its wings. Or perhaps it had flown without our seeing it. Perhaps at night. At night? It can't fly at night. Why not? That's just the way it is: it can't fly after dark; it's not a bat after all! The stationmaster fell silent: the other two were beginning to annoy him. He took a few steps back from the window, then left the room. It was no longer raining outside.

He hadn't been in a town since Maria's funeral. She didn't want to be cremated at the sanatorium, or buried in the village nearby, so they had to carry her to the next stop on the other side of the forest, and from there by train. But first there had to be an autopsy: the people at the hospital absolutely insisted on it, in the interests of science; anyway, they said, it won't make any difference to you. He agreed in the end, sat down on a bench in the clearing opposite the hospital, and waited for science to take a little step forward. Manolache came along to help, while Luca remained alone at the station. Then things started to move more quickly: the other stop wasn't far, and from there it was only an hour by train to the first small town. The burial was done with great speed, with just the two of them plus the priest and gravediggers in attendance. They could even return the same day, in the evening, carrying a crateful of rum bottles and a pack of cards.

Winter set in. The rain turned to sleet and snow, and soon the white flakes had covered everything. It snowed almost every day, and special teams came twice to clear the line; the ploughs attached to the locomotives were often powerless. It was around then that the accident occurred. It wasn't one of those disasters you read about in the papers: only two people died, later at the hospital, while a few more came out of it with injuries of varying severity. Nor was it anyone's fault. The train derailed at a bend where the wind had piled up a snowdrift; thick flakes were still falling, so that the engineer could see only a white wall ahead. He wasn't going particularly fast, but at that point the line must have been covered with a crust of ice. It would have been terrible if they hadn't managed to stop the express that was just behind the freight train; it had left the last station before their stop and, defying the snow, was racing like crazy to make up lost time, but the engineer noticed the stop signal and braked just in front of their little station, where the three railwaymen, headed by the tall mustachioed stationmaster, were standing in a state of great agitation. Faces appeared at the carriage windows, more excited than upset. The falling snow looked so beautiful, and when the passengers heard what had happened—some said they'd be stuck there till evening—most decided to disembark. There had never been so many people on the platform! The stationmaster ran this way and that, not knowing what to do, while Luca chatted with the conductor. Manolache seemed to have vanished—but no, there he was in front of the freight shed, looking attentively and no doubt bashfully at the crowd of elegant strangers. Some went into the office and, not finding anyone there, came out again; when they saw the stationmaster wandering aimlessly on the platform, his cherry-colored cap pulled tight over his head, a few went up to him and asked if there was anything to drink. Manolache! he shouted, and the last bottles of rum were made available. Others filled in time by taking a walk, enchanted by the forest landscape; some even had skis, and the younger and bolder among them, following Manolache's directions, went a few hundred meters down the forest track that led to the sanatorium. Only the tall beautiful woman with long blond hair, wearing a white pullover and blue pants, who spoke neither Romanian nor French (Luca said she was Swedish, in the long discussions the men later had among themselves), was initially unwilling to get off the train and preferred to stay in her compartment; the cage that the boss would later carry down the long sleeping-car wagon lay on the top bunk, while she sprawled on the lower one, waiting calmly with her hands crossed behind her neck. She got up a couple of times and went to the window in the corridor— once as the stationmaster was passing—then returned to the compartment, looked for a few moments at the baby eagle that was pecking at the bars of the cage, and lay down in the same position as before. The other passengers were fretfully walking up and down or discussing among themselves in motley groups. The train naturally had a dining car, but there wasn't enough space at lunchtime when everyone suddenly became ravenous; food had to be taken into the waiting room or even the station bedrooms, to which the three hospitable members of staff had no objection. Thick powdery snowflakes continued to fall. The prevailing gaiety was rather inappropriate, given the reason for the unscheduled stop, but no one seemed to give it a second thought. Lunchtime also saw the blonde lady alight from the train: now she stepped down onto the platform without hesitating (she was used to even worse snow in Sweden, Luca explained the next day) and went straight to the stationmaster, who stood out because of his red cap and solid, athletic figure. He had no way of understanding what she said, and, finding himself unexpectedly face-to-face with her, he could do no more than nervously twirl his mustache. Sign language didn't help. She bent her knees slightly and spread her long arms like wings, then drew them back and tried to indicate something small with her hands, before opening her arms wide again and flapping them several times. She's round the bend, the man said to himself, and he gently tugged at his chin. Maybe you want to eat, he said, tapping two fingers against his lips and moving them down to his stomach, but she continued to alternate between flapping her arms and leaning toward him to indicate something small: a cup, a snake, a bird, he couldn't figure it out. Then she took him by the hand and led him into the train, climbing up in front of him as he admired the shape of her legs and hips in her tight blue pants. He followed her along the corridor and into her compartment, where she turned and flashed him a smile.

He took a few steps toward the forest, then stopped. The earth was steaming from all the rain, and here and there his boots sank up to their laces in mud. The shrieking of the birds put his senses on edge: their short and long cries pierced the even rustle of the waves of leaves; a strange panting sound came from under the ground. In the distance he could hear moans interlaced with growls and grunts, a continuous grinding of teeth, persistent scratching sounds, and above everything an owl's hoots, a woodpecker's rattle, and a wolf's raucous howls, then a moment or two of silence broken only by the monotonous rustling of leaves, before the noise started up again and little wings flapped in fear. It was best to turn back. He had spent nearly all night sitting up at Manolache's bedside, and now he had a headache. The old man's dying, he said to himself, there's not much longer to go—and just then he heard a powerful beating of wings above the forest, and a shadow fell over the trees. How big it's grown, the stationmaster whispered, and all he could now hear was the rustling of leaves; the eagle must have landed in the clearing in front of the sanatorium, where Luca thought they should take the old man; but how were they to get him there, the path was basically nonexistent, and you know what, Luca—he moved closer to the young clerk, his eyes glistening from emotion or from fear—I don't think they're still taking people at the sanatorium, I mean, it was already old and in need of repair ... Bullshit! Luca said, and he looked at the old man, sighing softly, one hand glued to his chest, the truth is that you're afraid. The stationmaster made no answer: only later, after the express had passed through and the fine rain had begun rattling again on the tin roof of the shed, and when the old man had fallen asleep and was breathing a little more easily, did he take Luca aside and ask him to get on the first train and try to fetch a doctor. There's no point phoning, you have to go there yourself; you're a smart kid, you'll find some way. Please go, will you? We can't carry him anywhere in this state; we'll see how he is later ... He was surprised that Luca agreed so readily, so hastily even. The next night was torture: the old man thrashed about on the bed, groaning in his sleep, or woke up and began to speak without rhyme or reason, although now and again a phrase or two made some sense. Most of it was about his youth as a circus acrobat, about a lion that flew above him or fell on top of him, so that they both slid down into a well full of stars. The old man's face became completely distorted in the effort to speak, to bare his heart . . . But nothing could be done to help him.

He turned back toward the station, trying as hard as he could to avoid sinking into the mud. Again he heard the sounds of the forest, which seemed even louder than before: the shrill cries of the birds and the dull floundering of bodies as they slid, dashed, or crept between the tree trunks. He couldn't refrain from turning his head sharply. There was no one behind him, nothing special to be seen.

There in the corner, the old man groaned, look, there it is— and he pointed with his emaciated arm to a creature that he alone could see. The vigil-keeper wiped the perspiration from the old man's brow, took the glass of water from the table, and propped him up so that he could drink. No, I'm not afraid, I promise you I'm not. Why should you be afraid? the other man said, you just have to be patient a little longer. And outside the fine rain was still pelting onto the roof and the oak leaves, and onto the rails where not a single train had passed for twelve hours. Toward morning the old man finally fell asleep, one hand on his chest, the other clutching the side of the bed. The rain had stopped; dawn was breaking. He went into the telegraphy room, pulled one lever and then another, flicked one switch and then another: nothing, the telegraph was silent. He dropped his head onto his arms and remained like that for a time, without thinking. He felt that he was sinking into a wet, pitch-black darkness, or else rising to the surface from below like a drowned man.

It wasn't easy to carry the cage through the narrow sleeping car, even though the carriage was empty. Some of the passengers were still walking around the platform or behind the station— the boldest had gone with skis along the path into the forest— while others were seated over lunch in the waiting room or Luca's bedroom, since there wasn't enough space in the dining car. The cage knocked against the sides of the corridor, making the bird frightened and flustered; it tried to open its wings and pecked at the bars or at the man's thigh, which fortunately was clad in the thick blue material of his railroad uniform. The woman followed behind, and whenever he turned his head she immediately put on the enigmatic smile she had worn shortly before in the compartment; he had become awkward and tried to kiss her, but then realized that he was being ridiculous; her smile seemed automatic, as if all you had to do was push a button and a little pink light would come on behind her brow and light up her face and blue eyes. She had pointed to the cage and uttered something in that harsh language of hers: a few short words, spoken in a husky, peremptory voice. He looked at the cage, then at her, and nodded dutifully, feeling sheepish because of what he had done a moment earlier. She pulled his jacket sleeve and raised his arm toward the cage: this time he got the message, or thought he did, and so he stood on tiptoe, took the cage with gilded bars (or were they perhaps really golden?), and went out with it into the corridor. The woman smiled at him. He took the cage up to his room, watched with surprise by Luca and the old man, then went to look for some water and meat. The eagle was thirsty; it nearly broke the bowl as it plunged its curved beak inside.

It had been raining for days—fine raindrops pelting down without a break. The clouds were still closely packed, neither very high nor very low, as if there was only one, a huge grayish-white belly; it was raining, and the oak tree to the right of the shed was bloated with water, its leaves motionless and as heavy as lead. Not a single train had passed through for ages: Luca hadn't returned; there was no way he could have. From time to time he went out onto the platform, huddled in his waterproof coat, carrying that ragged piece of flag by force of habit, no doubt, and there he would stand for a long time motionless and look absently down the rails.

He was waiting. The old man had died with his eyes fixed on a corner of the room, having raised his head in a final effort, trying vainly to reach out his arm; his head had fallen onto the pillow, while one hand curled tightly around his cotton shirt. The boss had lain his other hand next to it before closing his eyelids and opening the window: the sky seemed to have brightened a little.

He went into Luca's office and sat on his chair, in front of the desk with all that complex equipment covered in dust. He pulled a lever, flicked a switch, then gave up. When they had heard that the local train was being withdrawn, they had angrily begun to draft a memorandum many pages long and ended up arguing over it. It had been a real battle: Luca had said he was leaving, that he would hand in his resignation. He flew off the handle, didn't know what he was saying, but he hadn't been right, no, Manolache agreed that he hadn't. The proof was that they didn't send any memorandum in the end; it would have been pointless, maybe no one would even have read it, and well, even if they had, what do you think could have been done about it: once something's decided, that's how it remains. There's nothing we can do, and Luca muttered too: nothing we can do, no, nothing, Manolache echoed cheerily. In the room all that could now be heard were the fine raindrops, that monotonous, irritating pitter-patter, and the panting breath of the dying man. And yet the clouds looked thinner than before, no longer so closely packed. A rosy light glowed in a patch of sky above the forest. He gripped the window ledge and waited.

It was snowing outside. At some point the rain had turned to sleet and snow, and the white flakes had soon covered everything. It snowed almost every day, as it had in the winter of the accident. It wasn't a disaster like you read about in the papers, nor was it anyone's fault. A train's come off the rails at a bend: Luca had shouted it at the top of his voice, but although he heard it the first time he cupped his hand around his ear and leaned out the upstairs window. A freight train's come off the rails, Luca shouted again, and the express will have to stop here till we get instructions. Manolache picked himself up and stuck the spade in the heap of snow. The engineer noticed the signal in time and, although he was racing like crazy to make up lost time, he managed to brake just in front of the stop, where all three of the staff members were standing in a state of great agitation. It was snowing heavily, with thick flakes, but it was so beautiful that all the passengers climbed down onto the platform. Only she preferred at first to remain in her compartment: maybe she didn't know what had happened, maybe she didn't understand a word anyone said; she had a way of speaking that was husky and melodious at the same time, and he shrugged his shoulders: maybe she's hungry, then pointed to his mouth and his stomach, do you want to eat something? She bent her knees slightly and spread her long arms, flapping them several times, then leaned toward him and brought her hands close together to indicate she was referring to a snake or a bird—a baby eagle with moist round eyes that she kept in a cage with gilded bars, up there on the top bunk. He tried to kiss her, but he quickly realized that he'd misinterpreted the mysterious smile that shone on her face like a lightbulb when you flick a switch. It wasn't easy to carry the cage through the narrow sleeping car, even though it was now empty of passengers. The cage knocked against the doors and walls: it was heavy, and the eagle tried to spread its wings and to peck at the gilded bars or the thigh of the man in blue railroad uniform. The woman had fallen behind, so he stopped and waited for her to catch up.

She was Swedish, Luca said as he dealt the cards; tall and blonde like that, with a white sweater, she couldn't have been anything else, so she must have been used to much worse snow. That's why she was in no hurry to get out, and when she decided to she was cool as a cucumber, not even taking much interest in her surroundings. I bet you anything you like she was Swedish.

The other two said nothing. Don't you agree? Then, looking surprised, with the rest of the cards in his hand, he sounded it out: Sweeeedish, that's what she was. Come on, forget your theories and deal, the man with the mustache said, casting a glance at the cage, and Manolache, catching the glance, muttered that it had been a mistake to let the eagle go, we shouldn't have done it, I'm telling you. Then he hurried to the window. He was never wrong. Come here, he said, taking Luca by the arm: just look! Above the forest the sky was turning crimson, and after a while the eagle suddenly shot out, as big as an airplane, and began to fly around in wide circles, wider and wider circles, which took it above the station building. Has it grown some more? Luca asked, and it was clear he was a little afraid: not so much of the eagle and its unnatural rate of growth (maybe it's a giant species from Sweden!) as of the solemnity and barely concealed joy with which the other man followed the bird's increasingly frequent flights. Afterward, Manolache could no longer get out of bed, and the other two took it in turns to keep watch over him.

He took a few steps toward the forest and stopped. The earth was steaming from all the rain. He buried Manolache there, behind the building; he dug a deep grave, for fear that wolves might sniff out the corpse and try to get to it with their claws. He spent a whole morning digging in the rain. The shrill cries of birds in the forest pierced the rustling of leaves and the even, monotonous pitter-patter of the rain; in the distance he could hear groans mixed with growling and hissing, and the sound of little wings beating fearfully. A strange panting seemed to well up from under the ground. There too, as in the forest, a whole secret industry of factories and workshops worked tirelessly around the clock. He continued his walk at a gentle pace, no longer with any obligations, free from morning to night. He took a few deep breaths and thought for a moment of walking to the sanatorium— it would take three hours if he speeded up a little—or of explaining the situation to them over the phone: the old man's death, Luca's disappearance, the broken telegraph; there was so much to say, too much even for one conversation. And why didn't you report this earlier? What could he say? . . . He too had been ill: he'd probably caught a cold on the day he buried the old man, when he dug that really deep grave . . . And why did no more trains come by their stop? Now it was his turn to ask the questions, speaking in a gruff voice and clearing his throat severely. They'd done away with the stop and abandoned him there, in the back of beyond, although, quite frankly, the idea didn't terrify him—on the contrary, a joy for which he found no obvious justification rose from the depths of his being at the thought. He realized that he was happier than he'd been for a long time, perhaps more than ever before in his life. What point was there in going to the sanatorium as well? Who knows, perhaps it had been deserted for a long time and all he'd find would be some bare walls, a roof partly torn off by the wind, and birds nesting in the beams that were still intact; forest beasts would be prowling outside, even strolling undisturbed through the wards, between the beds, in the operating theater; the last patients would have given up the ghost as hot-breathed animals licked their fleshless hands and feet. And even if things were not like that, even if the sanatorium had been repaired and fitted with ultramodern equipment from abroad, even if patients were sunning themselves on the terrace in multicolored deckchairs under the watchful eyes of tall blonde nurses in white uniforms, even if the sanatorium was prospering and automobiles on the grass outside added another modern touch—even then, what was the point in his going there? He had to stay where he was, at the stop: he couldn't leave his post, although the telegraph was broken and no more trains ever came by—or perhaps, in the days and nights when he'd lain ill or been sleeping a lot to regain his strength, many trains had passed one after another for a week or a whole month?—anyway, he had to wait there, flag at the ready, right hand raised to his cap, always standing at attention.

It was snowing. Manolache was clearing the snow, his tapering fur hat pulled over his ears. He, meanwhile, was shaving in his room upstairs and calling down, good morning, Manolache. Above the forest, the sun had begun to clear a space for itself among the clouds. Then the accident happened, and the express was forced to stop at their platform. Nearly all the passengers climbed down from the carriages, as happy as larks. The large powdery snowflakes filled them with wonder. Later the blonde woman disembarked as well and began to flap her arms like wings, then led him back to her compartment, where he tried to kiss her. She didn't even push him away; maybe her smile was enough for him to realize how ridiculous he was being. He saw the cage and, for the time being, still didn't understand. Only much later, after the express had left and many nights had passed, after the old man had died and Luca, the talkative clerk, had disappeared—only then did things become clear.

It's been raining for days now—fine raindrops pelting down without a break. But soon the clouds will no longer be so closely packed that you'd think there was only one, a huge grayish-white belly; it's raining, and the oak tree to the right of the shed is bloated with water; its leaves are motionless, as heavy as lead. Not one train has passed for ages: in vain does the stationmaster stand on the platform in his waterproof coat, holding the soaked flag in his left hand, ready to raise the other to salute. No more trains pass by; grass and weeds have grown between the tracks, and the rails have started to rust.

Yet still he waits. He shaves carefully every day, puts on new clothes, and waits. Seated on a bench on the platform, he listens to the rustling of the forest, the sound of rain striking leaves, and now and then distant groans and cries. He looks for a long time at the wooded hills that surround the stop. Sometimes the rain gives up for a while, part of the sky begins to turn rosy, and all the lesser sounds are covered by the flutter of huge wings. Then he gets up from the bench and, standing straight, his throat dry with emotion, follows the circle or spiral of the eagle's flight. His face glows, as if in ecstasy, and his fingers grip the flag shaft or the blue cloth of his uniform. It won't be much longer. He'll wait patiently, always at the ready. Then the rain will stop, the clouds will crumble and flee with the wind, and a clear blue sky will remain. He will once more get up at daybreak, his eyes sparkling with joy. In the mirror his smile will be as intense and enigmatic as that of the woman in the train. He will shave, rub on some perfume, meticulously brush his clothes (which look almost new, though of late he's been wearing them every day), take his cherry-colored cap from on top of the cage, and go out onto the platform. He will enter Luca's office, look at the dusty telegraph, then go to the window and see a part of the sky known only to him turn rosy. He will go out, take a few steps toward the dense verdure, and listen to the rustling of leafy waves and the shrieking of birds; he will hear all the distant groans and cries and panting sounds, which seem to come from under the ground, or rather from the forest depths. He will turn back, look over to the hill facing the stop, and take in the rusty rails overgrown with grass and weeds; he will sit down on the bench and wait, his eyes fixed on the sky.

There, above the forest, the sky will continue to color: rose will gradually turn into red, getting brighter, stronger, a crimson red, an imperial red!—and then all the forest sounds will grow softer, until all that can be heard will be the silvery wings of the eagle fluttering free above the treetops, huge now and covering the hills and forest with its shadow; it will soar higher and higher, a silver gleam against the crimson silk of the sky, circling once, twice, countless times, first ascending, then descending, and the circles, ever wider, ever slower, will pass above the stop, above your face transfigured with emotion, your dry throat, your eyes moist with joy, and the muscles of your neck hurting from the strain of following the eagle's ever wider, ever lower flight, and at some point a shadow falls over everything, but you, with mechanical gestures, begin to unbutton your uniform and shirt, the eagle flies ever lower, ever closer, its swishing wings thrash the air, the branches of the trees bend, the oak's right down to the ground, and the station roof is torn off, all is dark and cold, the silver wings closer, ever closer, you can no longer see the sky, the eagle is now your sky, and you thrust out your chest, your whole body, in one last effort.

But until then it rains nonstop—fine raindrops pelting down without a break . . .

At the Bottom of the Stairs

It wasn't complicated: the same movements, so long repeated, reflex actions, pushing a few buttons, turning some handle or other, flicking a switch, moving a lever, pushing, pulling, and turning, the same buttons, handles, switches, and levers, over and over again—no big deal at all. He could find them in the dark, like you find your mouth or nose or ears, always in the dark, but he had been making them all part of himself for such a long time. On the control panel a single light, a clear greenish eye, lay above a serrated switch that he only had to turn once in a while, with the lightest of touches, after which, for a few moments, he heard the tinkle of a bell and something like the whir of film rewinding. Pitch darkness, dense and recently a little damp. First—if there can be a first in a circular series of movements—he took three steps to his right and pressed an almost silky-smooth button with his middle finger; it had been sticking lately, and sometimes he had to press with his ring finger too. Next, another couple of steps right, where he flipped a switch two or three times—he couldn't have said when or why it was sometimes two, sometimes three—and then another switch a little higher, in line with his forehead, which he took between his thumb and index finger; he had to lift his arm to ear level and bend it more than for the other switches, because it was further up and needed greater force, and he felt too short and increasingly weak. Next he had to pull a handle, right, left, up and down, right, left, up and down, and wait; he didn't know for precisely how long, but he could tell when it was time to drop on his haunches and press three keys with three fingers, pausing a little between the first and the second—a triplet! Then back on his feet, two steps left, another button, a slight bending movement, an icy cold lever—it froze his hand—and sometimes, very infrequently, a quick turn of the serrated switch on the opposite side, beneath the greenish eye; its light was invisible to him, but he could feel its probing stare on his neck, perhaps sardonic, perhaps even mocking, sometimes only disdainful or, extremely rarely, compassionate. He turned on his heels and crept a few steps forward, squelching in a little puddle formed a short while ago, then took a deep breath—click-click, followed by the melodious whirring sound. He didn't have to be near the control panel all the time; there were quite long breaks when—except for the unpleasant duty of turning a huge wheel from which something, probably a long heavy chain, hung suspended and made a horrific screeching sound, while he pushed on the wheel with all his might and had to endure the screeching and whining, by turns high-pitched and hoarse, but always horrific—he had nothing much to do. Here and there a button to press or a switch to turn. He inched around in the dark, careful not to stray too far from the green eye, so that he could be back when he felt the time had come to start work again, pushing, pulling, and turning the same buttons, switches, handles, and levers, with always the same reflex actions; time to return to the place from which, later, in three precisely calculated steps, he reached the button as silky-smooth as wrist skin, took another two steps to flip the switches up and down, lifting his arm to ear level, then the lever, then a pause, then down on his haunches: a press of his index finger on the three keys, a pause, and almost at once the other two, the middle and ring fingers, as on a piano. And again pushing and turning, up and down, right and left, countless buttons, handles, switches, and keys, and now and again the switch beneath the green sardonic eye. He also had time to walk around, taking long slow strides, knees slightly bent, avoiding puddles here and there; after he pushed on the wheel, he went for a walk and thought that for some time now things had been much easier. He didn't put it quite like that, because the some time was immeasurable, but anyway the work was clearly easier. Before, instead of a control panel with silky buttons and simple switches, there had been heavy levers, pulleys, and wheels as on a ship; he had had to use his whole body to twist massive cables smelling of rust, to push and pull steel rods with his chest, and to duck the hot pipes winding endlessly just above his head, in an atmosphere that was now dry and stuffy, now damp and hot, and in an endless darkness unrelieved even by the green eye, and alive with foul odors. True, he hadn't worked alone in those days. Little by little, the pulleys, wheels, and pipes were replaced with this control panel; the green eye began to glow, and in the end only a single wheel remained, the one controlling the well; he wasn't even sure he needed to struggle with it as much as he did. The work became easier, but he was alone and deprived of the pleasure he had discovered one day when he had climbed an endless rough stone staircase—the pleasure of looking through a hole the size of an ear, or even smaller, and seeing light, colors, and part-bodies dancing to music, faint but still music, from afar. As there were two of them then, one of them could always steal off when the work only required one pair of arms and crawl on all fours up the narrow, almost vertical, stairs; he could feel the cold uneven stone against the palms of his hands as he approached the slit of pale light. It was a grayish light, as dull as the colors that fluttered for a few moments to the rhythm of the faint distant music: a washed-out field green, a yellow as pale as a grated lemon, a whitish pink like the skin at the joints; and, now and then, blue strips of sky that flashed for no more than a second, again followed by whitish gray and pink, slow distant music, and part-bodies dancing to the rhythm. He couldn't stay long and hurried back down on all fours, because he was needed to help move the huge wheel linked to invisible chains and pulleys and, somewhere overhead, among the chains, to huge snakes of burning-hot cast iron; he couldn't calculate how far overhead, since he had only dared to crawl up the stairs as far as the slit of light, which had appeared in a kind of vertical pipe so thick that his fingers didn't meet when he tried to hold it in his arms. It had been better like that, the two of them together. The other man's body bristled with rough bristles and sharp angles that dug into his shoulder or thigh, and he would sometimes clasp it fiercely with his long bony arms and clawlike fingers, but there wasn't time for such games: the pulleys, wheels, and levers, all that hot iron smelling of steam and rust, needed to be kept in motion. The chains that formed the pulleys kept disappearing one after another, and the remaining ones were increasingly difficult to handle; they had to pull with all their might, their two bodies hanging on the end of the chain. So there had been less and less time during which he could climb the rough stairs and look through the slit at the washed-out colors, but also at the bright-blue strips of sky, enjoy the distant sounds and shapes, the music and the parts of bodies that he figured must be dancing.

Those were troubled times. Left on his own, he often went for a walk and thought of those days, unable to say how long ago they had been; they were just some time in the past, that was all. Now there were even more puddles, and they were even noisier (that is, deeper), his steps were slow and measured, and he was careful not to wander too far from the green eye. He made the same movements as before—pushing, pulling, and turning buttons, handles, and switches, with simple movements of his hands or arms—but now he was alone. One day the last chain on which they had hung like bell-ringers disappeared, and however much he fought against it, his companion went up and out with the chain, dragged by a mysterious, implacable force. He clung to the other man's body, trying with all his strength to keep it and the chain from vanishing, but it was no use. He felt himself rising with them, but he was destined to remain behind in the darkness, alone in front of a control panel with countless buttons, levers, switches, and valves, facing the mocking look of the green eye that rarely, very rarely, also showed a glint of pity. He felt dragged upward and would not have let go if his head hadn't struck one of the burning-hot tubes. The blow—for someone or something had shaken the chain at that moment—sent him crashing to the ground, where he lay dazed, almost unconscious, for a long time. When he came around, all the chains and huge wheels as on a ship had disappeared; all that remained was the one controlling the well, which he turned in vain, sometimes vaguely hoping that the chain he could hear strike the concrete walls would bring his companion back. Everything else had been replaced with the superb panel and the dozens of buttons, switches, and levers that could easily be controlled with simple repetitive gestures—and, behind them, the green eye.

Alone. He no longer dared climb the steep stairs to look through the slit. But how he would have liked to catch another glimpse of the strips of sky and patches of pinkish-white skin, to hear the pleasant music in the distance, to make out a few of the dancing shapes through the haze! The green eye twinkled imperiously—it was time. He raced up to it, then took three steps to the right and pressed a smooth, almost silky button with his middle finger, adding the weight of his ring finger since it had been sticking recently, then took two more steps to the right, flicked the bottom switch a couple of times, and then the top one, raising his arm to ear level, after which he pulled a lever left and right, up and down, right and left and down, dropped on his haunches and pushed three knobs far in, stood up again, took two steps left, paused, pushed a button, two more left, a slight bending movement, then another button, the terribly cold handle of the lever, a control switch, another button, and another, a handle—always the same movements, reflexes by now, pushing, pulling, and turning, while behind him the green light glowed mocking, or merely ironical, very rarely compassionate.

DUMITRU TSEPENEAG is one of the most innovative Romanian writers of the second half of the twentieth century. In 1975, while he was in France, his citizenship was revoked by Ceauşescu, and he was forced into exile. In the 1980s, he started to write in French. He returned to his native language after the Ceauşescu regime ended, but continues to write in his adopted language as well.

A translator from Romanian, Spanish, German, French, and Italian, PATRICK CAMILLER has translated many works, including Dumitru Tsepeneag's *Vain Art of the Fugue*, *The Necessary Marriage*, and *Hotel Europa*.

MICHAL AJVAZ, *The Golden Age.*
The Other City.
PIERRE ALBERT-BIROT, *Grabinoulor.*
YUZ ALESHKOVSKY, *Kangaroo.*
FELIPE ALFAU, *Chromos.*
Locos.
IVAN ÂNGELO, *The Celebration.*
The Tower of Glass.
ANTÓNIO LOBO ANTUNES, *Knowledge of Hell.*
The Splendor of Portugal.
ALAIN ARIAS-MISSON, *Theatre of Incest.*
JOHN ASHBERY AND JAMES SCHUYLER,
A Nest of Ninnies.
ROBERT ASHLEY, *Perfect Lives.*
GABRIELA AVIGUR-ROTEM, *Heatwave*
and Crazy Birds.
DJUNA BARNES, *Ladies Almanack.*
Ryder.
JOHN BARTH, *LETTERS.*
Sabbatical.
DONALD BARTHELME, *The King.*
Paradise.
SVETISLAV BASARA, *Chinese Letter.*
MIQUEL BAUÇÀ, *The Siege in the Room.*
RENÉ BELLETTO, *Dying.*
MAREK BIEŃCZYK, *Transparency.*
ANDREI BITOV, *Pushkin House.*
ANDREJ BLATNIK, *You Do Understand.*
LOUIS PAUL BOON, *Chapel Road.*
My Little War.
Summer in Termuren.
ROGER BOYLAN, *Killoyle.*
IGNÁCIO DE LOYOLA BRANDÃO,
Anonymous Celebrity.
Zero.
BONNIE BREMSER, *Troia: Mexican Memoirs.*
CHRISTINE BROOKE-ROSE, *Amalgamemnon.*
BRIGID BROPHY, *In Transit.*
GERALD L. BRUNS, *Modern Poetry and*
the Idea of Language.
GABRIELLE BURTON, *Heartbreak Hotel.*
MICHEL BUTOR, *Degrees.*
Mobile.
G. CABRERA INFANTE, *Infante's Inferno.*
Three Trapped Tigers.
JULIETA CAMPOS,
The Fear of Losing Eurydice.
ANNE CARSON, *Eros the Bittersweet.*
ORLY CASTEL-BLOOM, *Dolly City.*
LOUIS-FERDINAND CÉLINE, *Castle to Castle.*
Conversations with Professor Y.
London Bridge.
Normance.
North.
Rigadoon.
MARIE CHAIX, *The Laurels of Lake Constance.*
HUGO CHARTERIS, *The Tide Is Right.*
ERIC CHEVILLARD, *Demolishing Nisard.*
MARC CHOLODENKO, *Mordechai Schamz.*
JOSHUA COHEN, *Witz.*
EMILY HOLMES COLEMAN, *The Shutter*
of Snow.
ROBERT COOVER, *A Night at the Movies.*
STANLEY CRAWFORD, *Log of the S.S. The*
Mrs Unguentine.
Some Instructions to My Wife.
RENÉ CREVEL, *Putting My Foot in It.*
RALPH CUSACK, *Cadenza.*
NICHOLAS DELBANCO, *The Count of Concord.*
Sherbrookes.
NIGEL DENNIS, *Cards of Identity.*

PETER DIMOCK, *A Short Rhetoric for*
Leaving the Family.
ARIEL DORFMAN, *Konfidenz.*
COLEMAN DOWELL,
Island People.
Too Much Flesh and Jabez.
ARKADII DRAGOMOSHCHENKO, *Dust.*
RIKKI DUCORNET, *The Complete*
Butcher's Tales.
The Fountains of Neptune.
The Jade Cabinet.
Phosphor in Dreamland.
WILLIAM EASTLAKE, *The Bamboo Bed.*
Castle Keep.
Lyric of the Circle Heart.
JEAN ECHENOZ, *Chopin's Move.*
STANLEY ELKIN, *A Bad Man.*
Criers and Kibitzers, Kibitzers
and Criers.
The Dick Gibson Show.
The Franchiser.
The Living End.
Mrs. Ted Bliss.
FRANÇOIS EMMANUEL, *Invitation to a*
Voyage.
SALVADOR ESPRIU, *Ariadne in the*
Grotesque Labyrinth.
LESLIE A. FIEDLER, *Love and Death in*
the American Novel.
JUAN FILLOY, *Op Oloop.*
ANDY FITCH, *Pop Poetics.*
GUSTAVE FLAUBERT, *Bouvard and Pécuchet.*
KASS FLEISHER, *Talking out of School.*
FORD MADOX FORD,
The March of Literature.
JON FOSSE, *Aliss at the Fire.*
Melancholy.
MAX FRISCH, *I'm Not Stiller.*
Man in the Holocene.
CARLOS FUENTES, *Christopher Unborn.*
Distant Relations.
Terra Nostra.
Where the Air Is Clear.
TAKEHIKO FUKUNAGA, *Flowers of Grass.*
WILLIAM GADDIS, *J R.*
The Recognitions.
JANICE GALLOWAY, *Foreign Parts.*
The Trick Is to Keep Breathing.
WILLIAM H. GASS, *Cartesian Sonata*
and Other Novellas.
Finding a Form.
A Temple of Texts.
The Tunnel.
Willie Masters' Lonesome Wife.
GÉRARD GAVARRY, *Hoppla! 1 2 3.*
ETIENNE GILSON,
The Arts of the Beautiful.
Forms and Substances in the Arts.
C. S. GISCOMBE, *Giscome Road.*
Here.
DOUGLAS GLOVER, *Bad News of the Heart.*
WITOLD GOMBROWICZ,
A Kind of Testament.
PAULO EMÍLIO SALES GOMES, *P's Three*
Women.
GEORGI GOSPODINOV, *Natural Novel.*
JUAN GOYTISOLO, *Count Julian.*
Juan the Landless.
Makbara.
Marks of Identity.

HENRY GREEN, *Back.*
Blindness.
Concluding.
Doting.
Nothing.
JACK GREEN, *Fire the Bastards!*
JIŘÍ GRUŠA, *The Questionnaire.*
MELA HARTWIG, *Am I a Redundant*
Human Being?
JOHN HAWKES, *The Passion Artist.*
Whistlejacket.
ELIZABETH HEIGHWAY, ED., *Contemporary*
Georgian Fiction.
ALEKSANDAR HEMON, ED.,
Best European Fiction.
AIDAN HIGGINS, *Balcony of Europe.*
Blind Man's Bluff
Bornholm Night-Ferry.
Flotsam and Jetsam.
Langrishe, Go Down.
Scenes from a Receding Past.
KEIZO HINO, *Isle of Dreams.*
KAZUSHI HOSAKA, *Plainsong.*
ALDOUS HUXLEY, *Antic Hay.*
Crome Yellow.
Point Counter Point.
Those Barren Leaves.
Time Must Have a Stop.
NAOYUKI II, *The Shadow of a Blue Cat.*
GERT JONKE, *The Distant Sound.*
Geometric Regional Novel.
Homage to Czerny.
The System of Vienna.
JACQUES JOUET, *Mountain R.*
Savage.
Upstaged.
MIEKO KANAI, *The Word Book.*
YORAM KANIUK, *Life on Sandpaper.*
HUGH KENNER, *Flaubert.*
Joyce and Beckett: The Stoic Comedians.
Joyce's Voices.
DANILO KIŠ, *The Attic.*
Garden, Ashes.
The Lute and the Scars
Psalm 44.
A Tomb for Boris Davidovich.
ANITA KONKKA, *A Fool's Paradise.*
GEORGE KONRÁD, *The City Builder.*
TADEUSZ KONWICKI, *A Minor Apocalypse.*
The Polish Complex.
MENIS KOUMANDAREAS, *Koula.*
ELAINE KRAF, *The Princess of 72nd Street.*
JIM KRUSOE, *Iceland.*
AYŞE KULIN, *Farewell: A Mansion in*
Occupied Istanbul.
EMILIO LASCANO TEGUI, *On Elegance*
While Sleeping.
ERIC LAURRENT, *Do Not Touch.*
VIOLETTE LEDUC, *La Bâtarde.*
EDOUARD LEVÉ, *Autoportrait.*
Suicide.
MARIO LEVI, *Istanbul Was a Fairy Tale.*
DEBORAH LEVY, *Billy and Girl.*
JOSÉ LEZAMA LIMA, *Paradiso.*
ROSA LIKSOM, *Dark Paradise.*
OSMAN LINS, *Avalovara.*
The Queen of the Prisons of Greece.
ALF MAC LOCHLAINN,
The Corpus in the Library.
Out of Focus.
RON LOEWINSOHN, *Magnetic Field(s).*
MINA LOY, *Stories and Essays of Mina Loy.*

D. KEITH MANO, *Take Five.*
MICHELINE AHARONIAN MARCOM,
The Mirror in the Well.
BEN MARCUS,
The Age of Wire and String.
WALLACE MARKFIELD,
Teitlebaum's Window.
To an Early Grave.
DAVID MARKSON, *Reader's Block.*
Wittgenstein's Mistress.
CAROLE MASO, *AVA.*
LADISLAV MATEJKA AND KRYSTYNA
POMORSKA, EDS.,
Readings in Russian Poetics:
Formalist and Structuralist Views.
HARRY MATHEWS, *Cigarettes.*
The Conversions.
The Human Country: New and
Collected Stories.
The Journalist.
My Life in CIA.
Singular Pleasures.
The Sinking of the Odradek
Stadium.
Tlooth.
JOSEPH McELROY,
Night Soul and Other Stories.
ABDELWAHAB MEDDEB, *Talismano.*
GERHARD MEIER, *Isle of the Dead.*
HERMAN MELVILLE, *The Confidence-Man.*
AMANDA MICHALOPOULOU, *I'd Like.*
STEVEN MILLHAUSER, *The Barnum Museum.*
In the Penny Arcade.
RALPH J. MILLS, JR., *Essays on Poetry.*
MOMUS, *The Book of Jokes.*
CHRISTINE MONTALBETTI, *The Origin of Man.*
Western.
OLIVE MOORE, *Spleen.*
NICHOLAS MOSLEY, *Accident.*
Assassins.
Catastrophe Practice.
Experience and Religion.
A Garden of Trees.
Hopeful Monsters.
Imago Bird.
Impossible Object.
Inventing God.
Judith.
Look at the Dark.
Natalie Natalia.
Serpent.
Time at War.
WARREN MOTTE,
Fables of the Novel: French Fiction
since 1990.
Fiction Now: The French Novel in
the 21st Century.
Oulipo: A Primer of Potential
Literature.
GERALD MURNANE, *Barley Patch.*
Inland.
YVES NAVARRE, *Our Share of Time.*
Sweet Tooth.
DOROTHY NELSON, *In Night's City.*
Tar and Feathers.
ESHKOL NEVO, *Homesick.*
WILFRIDO D. NOLLEDO, *But for the Lovers.*
FLANN O'BRIEN, *At Swim-Two-Birds.*
The Best of Myles.
The Dalkey Archive.
The Hard Life.
The Poor Mouth.

The Third Policeman.
CLAUDE OLLIER, *The Mise-en-Scène.*
Wert and the Life Without End.
GIOVANNI ORELLI, *Walaschek's Dream.*
PATRIK OUŘEDNÍK, *Europeana.*
The Opportune Moment, 1855.
BORIS PAHOR, *Necropolis.*
FERNANDO DEL PASO, *News from the Empire.*
Palinuro of Mexico.
ROBERT PINGET, *The Inquisitory.*
Mahu or The Material.
Trio.
MANUEL PUIG, *Betrayed by Rita Hayworth.*
The Buenos Aires Affair.
Heartbreak Tango.
RAYMOND QUENEAU, *The Last Days.*
Odile.
Pierrot Mon Ami.
Saint Glinglin.
ANN QUIN, *Berg.*
Passages.
Three.
Tripticks.
ISHMAEL REED, *The Free-Lance Pallbearers.*
The Last Days of Louisiana Red.
Ishmael Reed: The Plays.
Juice!
Reckless Eyeballing.
The Terrible Threes.
The Terrible Twos.
Yellow Back Radio Broke-Down.
JASIA REICHARDT, *15 Journeys Warsaw*
to London.
NOËLLE REVAZ, *With the Animals.*
JOÃO UBALDO RIBEIRO, *House of the*
Fortunate Buddhas.
JEAN RICARDOU, *Place Names.*
RAINER MARIA RILKE, *The Notebooks of*
Malte Laurids Brigge.
JULIÁN RÍOS, *The House of Ulysses.*
Larva: A Midsummer Night's Babel.
Poundemonium.
Procession of Shadows.
AUGUSTO ROA BASTOS, *I the Supreme.*
DANIËL ROBBERECHTS, *Arriving in Avignon.*
JEAN ROLIN, *The Explosion of the*
Radiator Hose.
OLIVIER ROLIN, *Hotel Crystal.*
ALIX CLEO ROUBAUD, *Alix's Journal.*
JACQUES ROUBAUD, *The Form of a*
City Changes Faster, Alas, Than
the Human Heart.
The Great Fire of London.
Hortense in Exile.
Hortense Is Abducted.
The Loop.
Mathematics:
The Plurality of Worlds of Lewis.
The Princess Hoppy.
Some Thing Black.
RAYMOND ROUSSEL, *Impressions of Africa.*
VEDRANA RUDAN, *Night.*
STIG SÆTERBAKKEN, *Siamese.*
Self Control.
LYDIE SALVAYRE, *The Company of Ghosts.*
The Lecture.
The Power of Flies.
LUIS RAFAEL SÁNCHEZ,
Macho Camacho's Beat.
SEVERO SARDUY, *Cobra & Maitreya.*

NATHALIE SARRAUTE,
Do You Hear Them?
Martereau.
The Planetarium.
ARNO SCHMIDT, *Collected Novellas.*
Collected Stories.
Nobodaddy's Children.
Two Novels.
ASAF SCHURR, *Motti.*
GAIL SCOTT, *My Paris.*
DAMION SEARLS, *What We Were Doing*
and Where We Were Going.
JUNE AKERS SEESE,
Is This What Other Women Feel Too?
What Waiting Really Means.
BERNARD SHARE, *Inish.*
Transit.
VIKTOR SHKLOVSKY, *Bowstring.*
Knight's Move.
A Sentimental Journey:
Memoirs 1917–1922.
Energy of Delusion: A Book on Plot.
Literature and Cinematography.
Theory of Prose.
Third Factory.
Zoo, or Letters Not about Love.
PIERRE SINIAC, *The Collaborators.*
KJERSTI A. SKOMSVOLD, *The Faster I Walk,*
the Smaller I Am.
JOSEF ŠKVORECKÝ, *The Engineer of*
Human Souls.
GILBERT SORRENTINO,
Aberration of Starlight.
Blue Pastoral.
Crystal Vision.
Imaginative Qualities of Actual
Things.
Mulligan Stew.
Pack of Lies.
Red the Fiend.
The Sky Changes.
Something Said.
Splendide-Hôtel.
Steelwork.
Under the Shadow.
W. M. SPACKMAN, *The Complete Fiction.*
ANDRZEJ STASIUK, *Dukla.*
Fado.
GERTRUDE STEIN, *The Making of Americans.*
A Novel of Thank You.
LARS SVENDSEN, *A Philosophy of Evil.*
PIOTR SZEWC, *Annihilation.*
GONÇALO M. TAVARES, *Jerusalem.*
Joseph Walser's Machine.
Learning to Pray in the Age of
Technique.
LUCIAN DAN TEODOROVICI,
Our Circus Presents . . .
NIKANOR TERATOLOGEN, *Assisted Living.*
STEFAN THEMERSON, *Hobson's Island.*
The Mystery of the Sardine.
Tom Harris.
TAEKO TOMIOKA, *Building Waves.*
JOHN TOOMEY, *Sleepwalker.*
JEAN-PHILIPPE TOUSSAINT, *The Bathroom.*
Camera.
Monsieur.
Reticence.
Running Away.
Self-Portrait Abroad.
Television.
The Truth about Marie.